# Mahabharata

retold by Anupa Lal
Illustrated by Ishan

Wonder House

(An imprint of Prakash Books)

contact@wonderhousebooks.com



ISBN : 978-93-54405-33-4

# Author

Anupa Lal has been writing for children since she was a child herself, several decades ago.

Her first published book was a picture book titled *The Rescue*. She went on to write more books including collections of poems for children.

Retelling folktales has been another area of interest for her. She particularly enjoyed retelling *The Comic Capers of Sheikh Chilli*, which had been among her favorite stories as a child.

She has also retold stories of *Akbar and Birbal*, *Alladin*, *Sindbad the Sailor* and *Hatim Tai*.

Her latest book of fiction is *Oddbird*, the story of a girl just three inches tall who has been brought up happily by a family of pigeons.

Anupa Lal has written two biographies—*Shri Ramana Maharishi* and *Munshi Premchand*.

She has also translated several short stories by Munshi Premchand, from Hindi to English, as well as his last novel *Godan*.

Anupa Lal has been familiar since childhood with stories from the great epics of *Ramayana* and *Mahabharata*.

Retelling these magnificent stories for children has been a very moving and inspiring experience for her.

Besides writing for them, she enjoys interacting with children. She has visited several schools, in and around Delhi for storytelling and creative writing sessions.

# Contents

# Introduction

The Mahabharata is the story of a bitter dynastic struggle, which culminated in a war that almost wiped out the entire dynasty.

The word 'Maha' means great and 'Bharata' refers to the race of King Bharata, one of the illustrious ancestors of the royal house featured in this great Indian epic. Later the name 'Bharata' also came to be identified with India as a whole.

The Mahabharata is much more than just the history of the Bharata clan. Along with that other great epic, the Ramayana, it embodies the soul and spirit of India. Philosophy, myth and folklore, statecraft and the art of warfare, widen as well as deepen the central theme.

The Mahabharata is the longest literary work in the world, with more than two hundred thousands lines of verse. It is awe-inspiring in both scope and impact. Loved and revered in every corner of India, it has inspired the philosophic thought, the literature and the fine arts of many other countries besides India.

Composed in Sanskrit several thousand years ago, it retains the power to move us profoundly. Its superb and sensitive delineation of character,

its stirring action and its deep philosophy continue to be meaningful even today.

Rishi Vyasa, poet and philosopher, who is himself very much part of the story, is said to have composed the Mahabharata in his mind. He dictated it to Lord Ganesha, the elephant-headed god who overcomes all obstacles and who is propitiated at the start of every undertaking.

When it was complete, the gods in heaven heard Vyasa's poem. On earth, many years after the terrible war between the Kauravas and the Pandavas depicted in the Mahabharata, Arjuna's great-grandson King Janmejaya listened spellbound to the story of his forefathers recited by one of Vyasa's disciples.

Millions of men, women and children have heard or read the Mahabharata since then and been blessed by the beauty and the truth of this great work of art.

# 1. Bhishma's Solemn Vow

Hastinapur, situated in the ancient land of Bharata, was ruled by the illustrious Kuru kings of the lunar race. King Santanu—like his ancestors—was a noble warrior, loved and venerated by his people.

One day, riding beside the river Ganga, he saw a woman of rare beauty. Dressed in pale blue and adorned with gems, she shimmered like the sun-kissed waters of a stream. Santanu fell in love with this vision of beauty and asked her to be his queen.

'Gladly, my king,' she said. 'But on one condition. Promise me that you will never ask me who I am or question anything I do. The moment you break this promise, I will leave you.'

Captivated by the charm of this mysterious maiden, Santanu readily agreed to her strange request. They married within a few days, and she proved to be a loving wife and a virtuous queen. After a year of happiness, she gave birth to a healthy and beautiful son, heir to the throne of Hastinapur.

Santanu felt himself to be the happiest of men. However, that very night, the queen rose from her bed with the infant in her arms. Alone, she walked to the banks of the Ganga and threw the newborn into the deep, dark waters of the river.

The king was appalled at this inexplicable behavior, but did not utter a word. His lips were sealed. He had promised his queen never to question her. Despite what had happened, he loved her deeply and did not want to lose her.

Seven years went by, and each year the queen bore Santanu a healthy and beautiful son only to drown him in the river Ganga. When she was about to drown her eighth child, Santanu could no longer control himself. With tears of grief and anger, he asked why she was killing their children.

'You have broken your promise, my king, and I must leave you,' the queen said sadly. 'But hear my story before you judge me. I am not a mere mortal, I am the Goddess Ganga. Now that I have fulfilled my purpose on earth, I must return to heaven. The eight sons I bore you were the eight Vasus, heavenly beings cursed to be born in the world of men to atone for their sins. I have released seven of them from that curse and, this child, the eighth Vasu, needs to live a complete life here before returning to heaven.'

'He will be a worthy son to you, my king. I shall take care of him for a few years and then return him to you. Do not grieve. What was ordained has come to pass.'

With the baby in her arms, Ganga vanished from sight. Bewildered and desolate, Santanu returned to his empty palace.

Sixteen lonely years went by. Then, one day along the banks of the river Ganga, Santanu saw a strange sight. A handsome youth had held up the river's flowing water with a dam constructed of skillfully shot arrows. Santanu stood there watching the feat in awed silence and wonder when Goddess Ganga appeared before him, radiant as ever.

'Great king, it is time for you to meet your son, Devavrata,' she said. 'He is well versed in all the arts of a kshatriya warrior. Nobody will be equal to him in wisdom and prowess.'

Ganga returned to heaven as father and son embraced. With great joy Santanu took back his son. The people of Hastinapur rejoiced as Devavrata was crowned as the heir to the throne of the Kurus.

Fate intervened once again when Santanu fell in love with Satyavati, daughter of the chief of the fisherfolk. Her father however, would not agree to this union unless Santanu promised that Satyavati's son would become the heir.

Santanu could not deprive the valiant Devavrata of his birthright, so he refused. Yet, he was unable to forget Satyavati, and with time, he became increasingly distressed.

Devavrata discovered the cause of his father's unhappiness and took it upon himself to remove it. He renounced his right to the throne. He further vowed never to marry in order to ensure that there would be no other claimants to the throne. He undertook to live a life of perfect celibacy.

Gods in heaven showered flowers on the noble prince as he uttered the words that bound him to a life of sacrifice and loneliness. From then on, Devavrata was called Bhishma, he who unflinchingly fulfills the hardest of vows.

Santanu married Satyavati who gave birth to two boys—Chitrangada and Vichitravirya—heirs to the throne of Hastinapur.

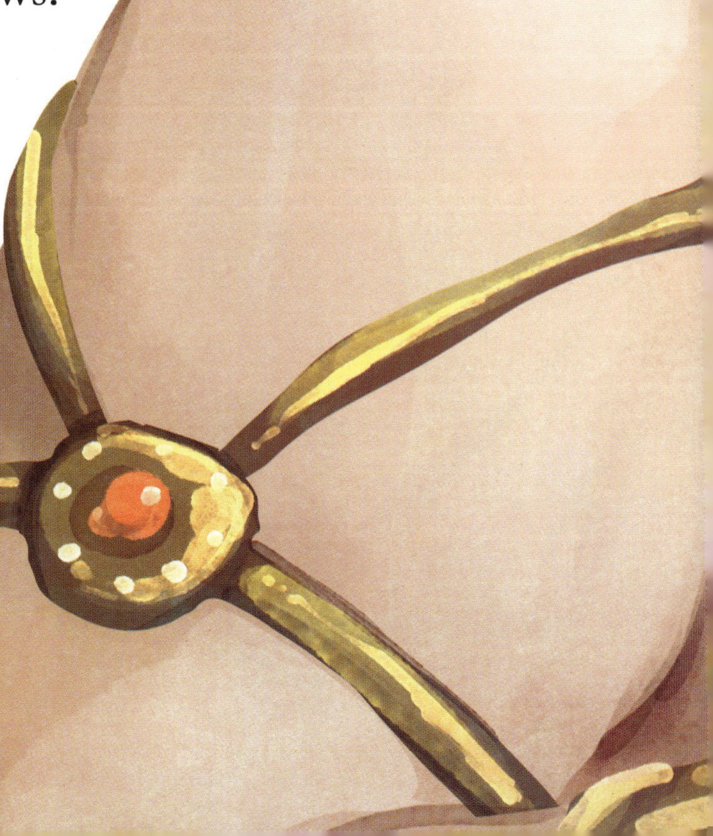

# 2. The Birth of Princes

Chitrangada, the elder son of Satyavati, ascended the throne of Hastinapur after the death of his father, King Santanu. A few years later, he died childless in a battle, and his brother Vichitravirya ascended the throne. As Vichitravirya was too young to rule, Bhishma governed the kingdom for him.

When Vichitravirya came of age, Bhishma won the three daughters of the king of Kasi as brides for him. Bhishma defeated all the other suitors by his superior skill at arms. The three princesses of Kasi were—Amba, Ambika and Ambalika. Before marrying Vichitravirya, Amba revealed her love for Salva, the king of Saubala. In her mind, she had already chosen him as her husband. Even though Bhishma had defeated King Salva in battle, he arranged for Amba to go to him with due respect and honor.

Still smarting from his defeat at Bhishma's hands, King Salva refused to accept her, and she returned to Hastinapur feeling baffled and humiliated. Amba entreated Bhishma to marry her. But he was bound by his vow of celibacy. Nor did Vichitravirya marry her as she had already given her heart to somebody else.

Amba's life was blighted for no fault of hers. All the love in her heart turned into fierce hatred for Bhishma. She held him responsible for ruining her life and appealed to all the renowned warriors of the land to fight Bhishma and avenge her but no one dared to do so. Even sage Parasurama, Bhishma's guru and a great warrior himself, could not defeat his pupil in single combat.

Frustrated at every turn, Amba turned to the gods. She practiced rigid austerities until Lord Shiva granted her a boon that in her next birth, she would be the cause of Bhishma's death. Years later, this came to pass.

Meanwhile, tragedy struck Hastinapur. Young king Vichitravirya died suddenly, leaving no heir to the throne. Traditionally, a son born to a noble brahmin could revive a noble line threatened with extinction. With this in mind, Queen Satyavati, the widowed mother of Vichitravirya, approached Vyasa, the great rishi. Vyasa was born to Satyavati and sage Parashara before she had met King Santanu.

In obedience to his mother's wishes, Vyasa fathered two sons that would be heirs to the throne of Hastinapur. The elder son Dhritarashtra, was born to Queen Ambika, and the younger son Pandu was born to Queen Ambalika. Vyasa fathered another son Vidura, who surpassed his brothers in wisdom, statesmanship and the practice of dharma. Dhritarashtra was born blind, so Pandu ruled the kingdom in his name with the assistance of Bhishma and Vidura.

When the princes reached adulthood, Bhishma arranged the marriage of Dhritarashtra with Gandhari, the virtuous daughter of the king of Gandhara. Not only did Gandhari willingly accept a blind husband, but she also bound her own eyes with a piece of cloth, forsaking the precious gift of sight that destiny had denied her husband.

Pandu married Kunti, the beautiful daughter of King Sura of the Yadavas. Following the prevailing custom, he took a second wife, Madri, sister to the king of Madra. Pandu was a great warrior. He established the supremacy of Hastinapur over all the kingdoms of Bharata, and the future looked bright. But once again, misfortune was to strike the Kuru race.

Once while hunting, Pandu shot a deer that was sporting in the forest with its companion. King Pandu was startled when he heard the deer he had shot utter a chilling human cry. In reality, the loving pair was a rishi and his wife.

‘O King, I curse you for this thoughtless and cruel deed,’ said the dying rishi. ‘You will never know the joys of fatherhood. You will die like me, the moment you enjoy the warm embrace of your wife.’

Heartbroken at this sudden calamity, Pandu lost all interest in his kingdom as now he could never give an heir to the Kuru dynasty. Renouncing all worldly possessions, he retreated to the forest with Kunti and Madri, leaving his blind brother Dhritarashtra as king.

The curse of the dying rishi continued to torment Pandu. He strongly desired sons and only Kunti had the power to relieve him of his suffering. When she was still a maiden, Sage Durvasa had spent a year as a guest in her father's palace. Kunti had served him with great care. Pleased by her devotion, the sage gave her a divine mantra by which she could invoke any god to bless her with a son equal to him in glory. Pandu's torment vanished when he learned about Kunti's boon.

He was overjoyed. He asked Kunti to invoke Dharmaraja, great Lord of Dharma, who blessed her with a son destined to win fame throughout the world for his righteous and noble conduct. He was named Yudhishthira. A year later, Kunti became the mother of another son, the strong and sturdy Bhima, born of the mighty Wind God, Vayu. Indra Deva, the Lord of the Heavens, blessed Kunti with a third son, Arjuna, destined to conquer the world and be invincible in war.

At Pandu's request, Kunti taught the divine mantra to Madri for she too wanted to beget children. By the grace of the Twin Gods, the Asvin Kumaras, Madri was blessed with beautiful twin sons—Nakula and Sahadeva. They grew up to be brave, handsome, and virtuous.

The day that Kunti's second son Bhima was born, Queen Gandhari gave birth to a boy named Duryodhana. In Hastinapur, evil omens attended this birth and prophesied widespread death and destruction.

'Sacrifice this child, my brother,' wise Vidura counseled Dhritarashtra. 'Save your kingdom from the carnage that will surely follow if he lives.'

But Dhritarashtra could not do so. Duryodhana was the eldest of a hundred sons and a daughter born to the blind and doting king.

In the forest, Pandu was elated to see the growth of his five god like sons. When Yudhishthira was barely sixteen, as the curse of the sage decreed, Pandu died in the arms of his second wife Madri. Entrusting her twin sons, Nakula and Sahadeva, to the care of Kunti, Madri burnt herself on Pandu's funeral pyre. The rishis of the forest escorted the grieving Kunti and her five sons to Hastinapur.

# 3. Duryodhana's Evil Plans

Hastinapur mourned the death of brave King Pandu. His funeral rites were performed with due honor by Rishi Vyasa and the elders of the Kuru house. Afterwards, Vyasa approached his mother Satyavati.

'Mother, there are dark days ahead,' he said gently. 'The great throne of the Kurus will be steeped in its own blood. Your great-grandsons are doomed to become enemies. Please leave this place before annihilation strikes and save yourself from the sorrows to come.'

Queen Satyavati was grief-stricken. She had dreamt many dreams of glory for Hastinapur, only to learn about its dreadful future. Accompanied by Ambika and Ambalika, she left the city and retired into the forest.

The Pandava princes, Pandu's sons, and the Kaurava princes, the hundred sons of Dhritarashtra, grew up together in the palace of Hastinapur. The palace resounded with the music of their laughter but it was already disturbed by notes of discord.

Duryodhana and his brothers harbored deep resentment for the Pandava princes. They most disliked Bhima, the strongest of all, who derived great pleasure from teasing them. Bhima would vigorously shake the trunk of any tree they climbed or would swim underwater while holding on to one or more of his wretched cousins till they almost drowned!

There was no malice in Bhima's teasing, but Duryodhana's resentment was founded on thwarted ambition. Although King Dhritarashtra was older than his brother Pandu, Pandu had ruled the kingdom for his blind brother. Yudhishthira was King Pandu's eldest son.

He was also a year older than Duryodhana. It was likely that he would be crowned the king of Hastinapur after Dhritarashtra, and not Duryodhana.

Neither father nor son could bear this possibility. While timidity and morality tempered Dhritarashtra's ambition for his son, Duryodhana's ambition was single-minded and powerful. He began to seek ways to remove the Pandavas from his path. The base thought of killing Bhima entered into his mind. He believed that Bhima's death would render the Pandavas weak and defenseless.

Bhima was well known for his prodigious appetite, and Duryodhana decided to take advantage of it. One day, when the Kaurava and Pandava princes had gone swimming in the Ganga, Duryodhana told Bhima that he had prepared a special banquet for him. He led him to an isolated place where the choicest dishes were laid out. Each one had been poisoned. Bhima enjoyed a hearty meal. As the poison began to work, he became very drowsy. He lay down and soon fell into a deep sleep. As Bhima lay asleep, Duryodhana bound him with creepers and threw him into the river. Sharp spikes had been planted at the spot where he was thrown in, to make Bhima's death a certainty.

Having been informed that Bhima had preceded them to the city, the Pandava and the Kaurava princes returned to Hastinapur. Duryodhana rejoiced inwardly confident that his most hated enemy was no more. But upon discovering Bhima's absence, the Pandavas hurried back to the river to search for him. He was nowhere to be found. Full of misgivings, the Pandavas returned to Hastinapur feeling dejected and lost.

Meanwhile, the unconscious Bhima had escaped the sharp spikes but was bitten all over by poisonous snakes. Their poison counteracted the poison he had consumed earlier, and miraculously he revived. After regaining consciousness, he returned home with increased vigor and strength. His mother and brothers embraced him with tears of joy. They suspected that Duryodhana had tried to kill Bhima. However, on Vidura's advice, they remained quiet so as not to fan the flame of hatred in Duryodhana's heart.

'Your sons have been blessed with long lives. Have no fear on their account,' far-sighted Vidura counselled Kunti. Bhima's return baffled Duryodhana. But he hid his true feelings and continued to scheme against his cousins.

Acharya Kripa, a sage well versed in the Vedas, had been appointed to educate the Kaurava and Pandava princes and train them in the arts of combat. As the princes grew older, their grandfather Bhishma sought a guru even more proficient than Acharya Kripa—someone to mold them into the finest kshatriyas—men of honor and invincible in war.

One fine morning, the princes were playing with a ball that suddenly fell into a nearby well. As they stood there, a lean and dark-skinned brahmin approached them. The brahmin asked what was wrong and they explained.

'Surely it should not be hard for skilled archers like you to retrieve your ball,' said the brahmin. 'And even this ring.' Taking a ring from his finger, he threw it into the well.

The Kaurava and Pandava princes were nonplussed. They watched the brahmin with wonderment as he took a long blade of grass, spoke a mantra over it and shot it into the well. It passed through the ring and pierced the ball like an arrow. He shot blade after blade, and all the blades combined to make a chain that pulled the ball and the ring out of the well.

Wonderstruck by the feat, the princes gathered around the brahmin, clamoring to know his identity. But all he said was, 'Go to your grandfather and tell him what you just saw. He will know who I am.'

He was Drona, son of the great sage Bharadwaja, husband of Acharya Kripa's sister Kripi. Like Bhishma, he was a gifted student of the warrior sage Parasurama, one of the greatest archers of all time.

Bhishma hurried out of the palace to welcome Drona. The search was over. He had found the ideal guru for his grandsons.

# 4. Invincible Archer Karna

Acharya Drona taught the many skills of warfare to the Pandavas and the Kauravas. His son, Aswatthama, joined the lessons. Arjuna, the third Pandava prince, was Drona's ablest student; his dedication and perseverance won the acharya's heart. Arjuna practiced archery till he could shoot as unerringly in the dark as in the day. Under Drona's tutelage, he learned how to fight on foot, on horseback, on the back of an elephant, and from a chariot. He could wield a spear, a mace, a sword, and a bow with equal proficiency.

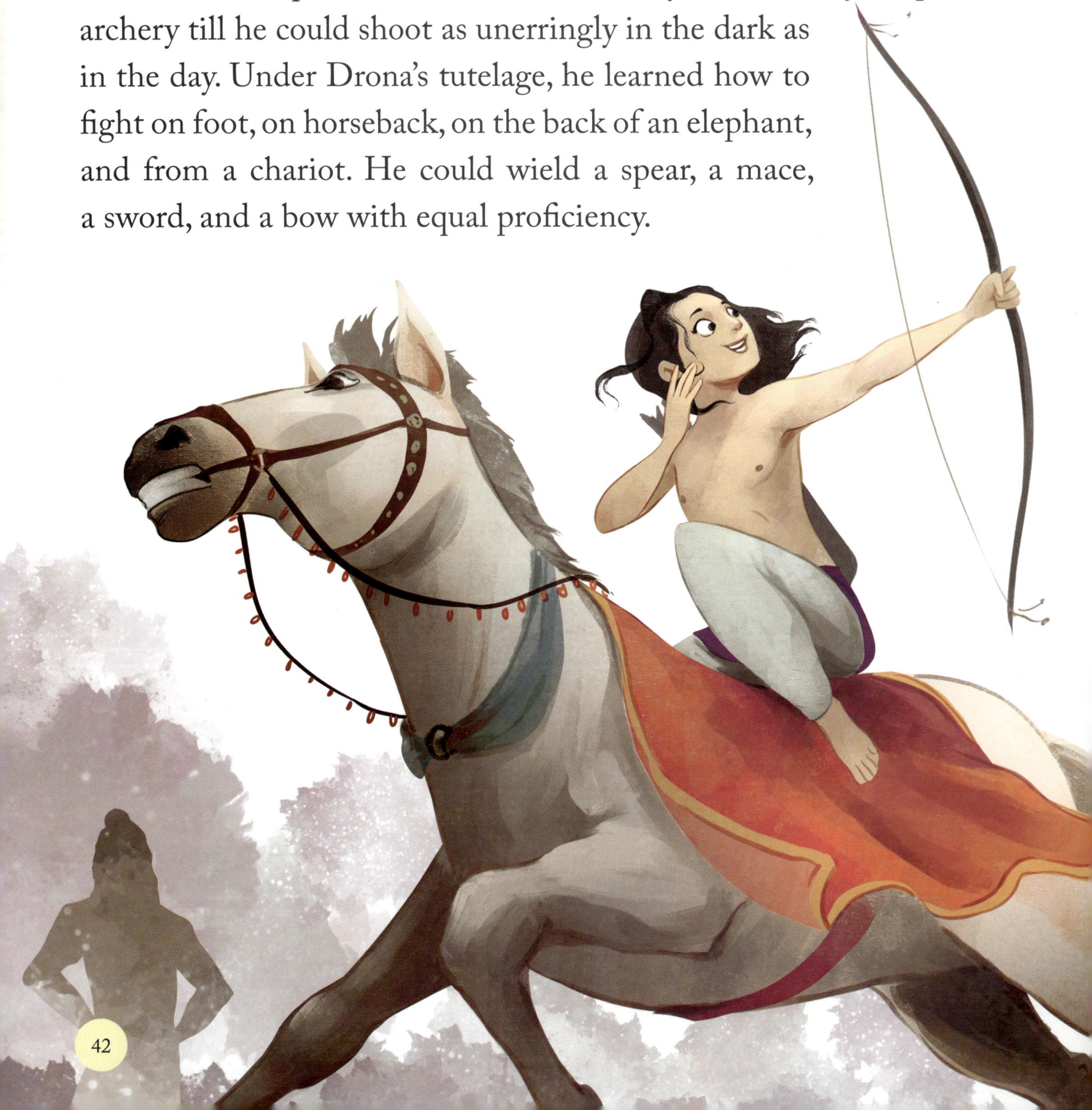

When the princes' training was over, Drona decided to test their archery skills. Placing a wooden bird high on a treetop, he instructed them to aim their arrows at its eye.

As Yudhishthira was ready to shoot, Drona asked, 'Tell me, what do you see?'

'I see the tree, Guruji. I see you and my brothers,' replied Yudhishthira.

'Enough,' said Drona. 'Your turn is over.'

Puzzled but obedient, Yudhishthira went back to his place. Drona put the same question to his other students. Each of them answered in much the same way as Yudhishthira and each was sent back without a trial of his skill.

Finally, it was Arjuna's turn. As he took careful aim at the target, Drona asked, 'My child, do you see your brothers watching you? Do you see me?'

'No, Guruji,' said Arjuna.

Everyone was mystified by Arjuna's answer except Drona, who remained unperturbed.

'Do you see the tree on which the bird sits?' he asked.

'No, Guruji,' said Arjuna again.

'Do you see the bird on the tree?' asked the acharya.

Arjuna's gaze was fixed on his target. Without turning his head he said, 'No, Guruji, I do not see the bird.'

'What do you see, my child?' asked Drona in a tender voice.

'I see the bird's eye, Guruji,' said Arjuna. 'I see my target.'

'Shoot it then!' Drona said triumphantly.

Arjuna's arrow flew through the air and directly hit the bird's eye. Drona embraced and blessed Arjuna.

'You have learned all that I could teach you,' he said. 'No archer on earth can match your skill.'

But Drona was wrong. There was a bowman, far superior to Arjuna. His name was Karna—destined to be Arjuna's most bitter rival.

Karna was born with gold armor encasing his tiny body and gold earrings glinting in his tiny ears. His beauty was as dazzling as the sun. But he could not receive the love of either of his parents. Abandoned in a wooden box set adrift on the river Ganga, he was found and adopted by a humble charioteer named Adiratha and his wife, Radha. Their love filled Karna's heart, but his spirit yearned for a higher destiny than that of a sutaputra, the son of a charioteer.

To gain proficiency in martial arts, he went to Drona, who accepted him as a pupil, but would not teach him the Brahmastra, the supreme weapon, since Karna was not of noble birth.

In desperation, Karna sought another guru to teach him the use of the Brahmastra. The great sage Parasurama became his guru, and after many years of intense training, he was finally able to learn how to use the divine weapon. Parasurama thought his pupil was a brahmin. When he discovered that Karna had lied to him about his birth, he was outraged.

'You have learned the Brahmastra from me by unfair means. I curse you!' he thundered. 'The divine weapon will fail you when you need it the most.'

Karna fell at his guru's feet and begged for mercy. Although Parasurama could not take back his words, he was deeply moved by Karna's distress and years of selfless service. He decreed that despite the curse, Karna would be remembered as the greatest archer that had ever lived.

The training of the Kaurava and Pandava princes drew to a close. So, Drona arranged a demonstration of their skills for the king, the nobility, and the residents of Hastinapur. Amidst the sounds of beating drums and blowing trumpets, Drona entered the arena clad all in white. He was as stately as the moon. The princes followed him, shining like stars. Bowstrings twanged, swords flashed, and maces thudded against their targets. But no feats could equal Arjuna's. His arrows created fire, thunderclouds, and rain. On foot, on horseback, erect, supine, in every posture, with every weapon—Arjuna outshone all his illustrious brothers and cousins.

The day was his. But before it was over, into the arena strode the only warrior who could challenge him. Tall, majestic Karna, resplendent in his armor of gold, bettered all Arjuna's feats with great ease and challenged him to single combat. The two young warriors faced each other like hungry lions and the crowd grew tense and excited.

Kunti, mother of the Pandavas, swooned when she recognized Karna. The sight of his golden armor and earrings—which were a gift from his father, the Sun God Surya—pierced her like an arrow. She had abandoned her firstborn child in the river Ganga out of immense shame and concealed the truth from her husband, Pandu. She bore Pandu five sons with the help of the divine mantra by which she could have the sons of any god, but the secret of her being a mother as a maiden and abandoning her beautiful baby boy still burned her heart.

'My son,' she murmured now as she looked at the handsome youth. Her heart was full of grief and longing but she did not dare to acknowledge Karna as her son.

Before Karna could fight Arjuna, Acharya Kripa asked him his lineage. According to age-old tradition, only princes could fight princes. Karna's proud face fell as a lotus wilts after heavy rain. Despite his prowess, he was only the son of a charioteer in the eyes of the world.

As he stood in silent dismay, Duryodhana came to his rescue and anointed him as the king of Angadesha. Now Karna was in no way inferior to Arjuna. It was a heaven-sent opportunity for Duryodhana to befriend Arjuna's adversary and win his undying affection and loyalty. The die was cast—brother pitted against brother. By the time Karna realized he was Kunti's eldest son, it was too late to change the course of events.

After the grand display of Hastinapur's secure future, it was now time for Drona to seek his guru dakshina. He first asked Duryodhana to capture King Dhrupada of Panchala and bring him alive as a traditional tribute to the guru. Duryodhana set out with his brothers to capture Dhrupada but returned empty-handed. It was Arjuna who succeeded in subduing the fiery king and brought him before Drona.

Drona looked at the man who was once his dearest friend. But wealth and power had changed him when he became king. He disowned the old friendship, declaring it possible only between equals, and reviled Drona as a penniless brahmin.

Not having forgotten the insult, it was now Drona's turn to tilt the scales of fortune in his favor. He returned Dhrupada half of his kingdom, retaining the other half to maintain equality and restore the broken friendship.

Friendship with Drona was the last thing King Dhrupada wanted. Burning with anger and humiliation, he vowed revenge and prayed to the gods for a son who would one day kill Drona and a daughter who would marry the great warrior Arjuna.

# 5. Draupadi's Swayamvara

The noble and accomplished Yudhishthira showed promise of becoming an ideal ruler. He was venerated by the people of Hastinapur, who wanted him to be their king. So, Dhritarashtra declared him heir to the throne. Duryodhana could not bear this. He persuaded his doting father to send the Pandavas away for a while so that he could win over the people and erase the image of the Pandavas from their hearts.

As uneasy as his son about the growing popularity of his nephews, Dhritarashtra went along with the plan. He asked Yudhishthira to go to the city of Varnavata with his mother and brothers to attend a great festival in honor of Lord Shiva.

Unknown to his father, Duryodhana's plan had a more deep and sinister purpose. He did not intend his cousins to return alive from Varnavata. Aided by his wily maternal uncle Sakuni, his friend Karna and his younger brother Dussasana, Duryodhana secretly instructed a minister named Purochana to build a beautiful but highly inflammable palace of wax at Varnavata. Later, Purochana would set it ablaze at an opportune moment, and the Pandavas would perish in it.

Vidura came to know of Duryodhana's evil plan and quietly warned Yudhishthira of the danger ahead.

'There are weapons deadlier than swords and arrows,' he said. 'Fire can burn down forests but it will not harm creatures who have burrowed deep into the earth. No harm comes to the alert man. The stars in heaven guide him on his way.'

Yudhishthira understood Vidura's warning. The Pandavas proceeded to Varnavata with heavy hearts. They moved into the palace, fully realizing that it was a death trap. But soon afterwards, Vidura secretly sent a miner to construct a tunnel underneath the inflammable dwelling as a means of escape.

The Pandavas were watchful of Purochana while living in Varnavata. They did nothing to arouse his suspicions. Then one night, before Purochana could cause them any harm, they set the palace on fire and escaped through the tunnel into the surrounding forest.

Word reached Hastinapur that the Pandavas had died in the devastating fire, but only Vidura knew the truth. The treacherous Purochana perished in the death trap of his own making.

For months, the Pandavas wandered through forest after forest, suffered many hardships, and braved many dangers. On the advice of their grandfather, Sage Vyasa, they sought refuge in the city of Ekachakra. Here they lived disguised as brahmins—begging for alms and sharing amongst themselves whatever they collected.

They repaid the hospitality of the people of Ekachakra when Bhima slaughtered a ferocious demon named Bakasura, who had terrorized them for many years.

While the Pandavas were in Ekachakra, they learned of the swayamvara of Draupadi, the daughter of King Dhrupada of Panchala. Draupadi was the daughter King Dhrupada had prayed for to Lord Shiva. She had arisen from the sacrificial fire, fully grown and as beautiful as a blue lotus. Her destiny awaited her, to wed the peerless bowman Arjuna.

From the same fire arose her brother Drishtadyumna, a warlike youth, fully-armed, and born to kill Drona—once his father's closest friend and now his most bitter enemy.

'Go to Draupadi's swayamvara,' Sage Vyasa told Yudhishthira and his brothers. 'Win her hand in marriage but stay disguised.'

The beautiful Panchala capital was alive with excitement. Illustrious kings from all corners of Bharata had gathered in the majestic marriage hall for the contest of skill organized by King Dhrupada for Draupadi's suitors.

Hoping against hope that the Pandavas were still alive, Dhrupada had devised a contest of skill which only an archer as accomplished as Arjuna could win. Draupadi's suitors had to string a mighty bow of steel and shoot five arrows through the aperture of a revolving disk at a moving target placed high above them.

In the august assembly were Duryodhana, Karna, Krishna-the chief of the Yadava clan, with his brother Balarama and many other great warriors. The five Pandavas also sat as and among the brahmins. The contest began, and each suitor strove to string the mighty bow, only to fail miserably. When Karna strung the bow, his arrows missed the target only by a hair's breadth.

When it seemed nobody could perform the task, Arjuna came forward and asked for permission to compete. Meditating on Vishnu, Lord of the Universe, he strung the magnificient bow with utmost ease. Five arrows were shot unerringly and brought the target to the ground.

The splendid hall rang with shouts of acclaim and the festive music of conches and trumpets. Draupadi joyfully placed the marriage garland around Arjuna's neck.

Many of the princes, including the Kauravas, were disgusted by the course of events. They were loath to see a brahmin win where they had failed and they sought to attack Arjuna. But they were no match for him and his brothers. The identity of the Pandavas was revealed to King Dhrupada. He was overjoyed. Draupadi's marriage was solemnized with pomp and ceremony.

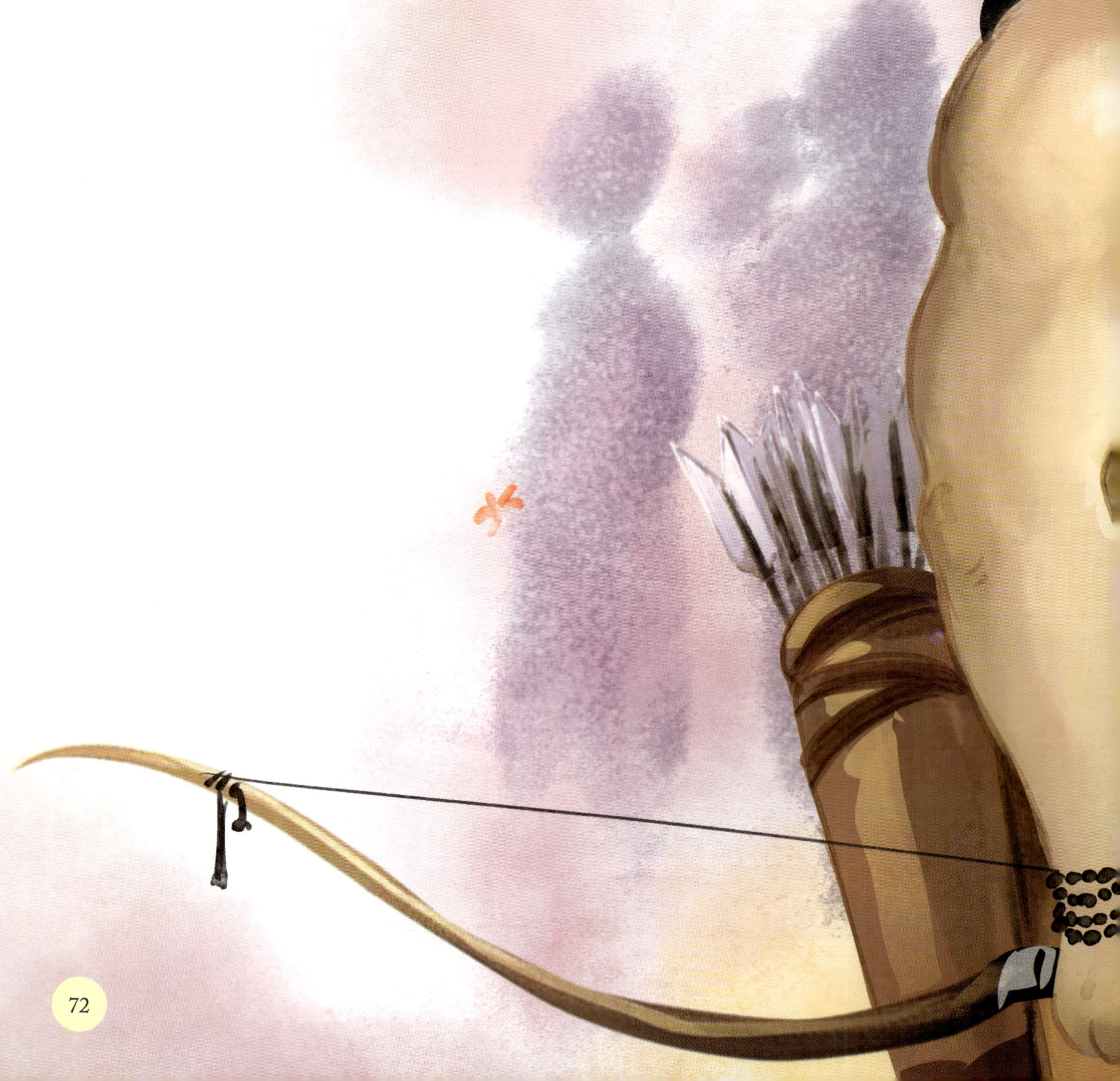

In a previous birth, Draupadi had obtained a boon from Lord Shiva that she would marry a man who was wise, virtuous, noble, powerful, invincible in war, and splendid to behold. In fulfilment of this boon, Draupadi married not just Arjuna but all the five Pandavas who together embodied all these virtues.

When Arjuna invoked Lord Vishnu before attempting to string the mighty bow, he was oblivious that the Supreme Lord was present in the court in the form of Sri Krishna. He was Kunti's nephew and therefore

cousin to the Pandavas. However, Arjuna's bond with Krishna went much deeper. It was the indissoluble bond between Nara and Narayana—the human and the divine, spanning a myriad lifetimes. Arjuna was yet to know of this bond.

After the swayamvara, Krishna and Balarama visited the Pandavas in their humble abode and expressed their delight at the wellbeing of Kunti and her sons.

# 6. Prosperous Indraprastha

Upon hearing the news that the Pandavas were alive and had allied with the powerful Dhrupada through their marriage to Draupadi, Dhritrashthra seemed very happy.

But he and his son Duryodhana were worried about the return of the Pandavas. Duryodhana, Karna, and Sakuni wished to crush the Pandavas once and for all, either by guile or open war. However, Dhritrashtra would not approve any such proposal without consulting his uncle, the patriarch Bhishma, Acharya Drona, and Vidura.

'Welcome your nephews,' Bhishma advised the king. 'And give them half of your kingdom. They have as much right to the throne as your sons. People suspect your hand in burning down the palace in Varnavata. Set their doubts at rest by dividing the kingdom equally between your sons and nephews and ensure justice.'

Drona and Vidura gave the same advice. As a result, Dhritrashtra sent for the Pandavas and welcomed them with open arms and tears of joy.

The people of Hastinapur rejoiced as the streets were sprinkled with water and decorated with flowers for the homecoming of their beloved Pandava princes. Yudhishthira was given half of the kingdom and crowned the king of Khandavaprastha.

Dhritrashtra had been unfair to his nephews in giving them a barren and deserted wasteland, unfit for habitation.

However, the Pandavas transformed Khandavaprastha into a beautiful and prosperous city-state with the guidance of Krishna and the help of the divine architect, Vishwakarma. It now contained the most exquisite palaces and forts, beautiful gardens full of songbirds, and shimmering pools adorned with lotuses. People thronged to the flourishing city—renamed Indraprastha. Its fame spread far and wide.

Yudhishthira ruled Indraprastha wisely for several years. Then on the advice of his councilors, he was persuaded to perform the Rajasuya sacrifice, which would establish him as the emperor of Bharata. Duryodhana, Karna, and Sakuni were among the large and distinguished assembly of kings who attended the grand ceremony and brought expensive gifts as tribute.

The prosperity and the power of the Pandavas filled Duryodhana with bitterness. After the guests had gone, he wandered through the splendid council hall, marveling at everything with envious eyes. Mistaking a pool of clear water for a marble floor, he stumbled into it,

and a peal of laughter from Draupadi mortified him further.

'Blind son of a blind father!' she said mockingly. The harsh words pierced Duryodhana's distraught heart like sharp arrows. He hastened back to Hastinapur full of rage and despair.

Duryodhana's evil mentor Sakuni, comforted him, 'Great prince, you are no less than Yudhishthira,' he said. 'Why this grief and despair? Do not think of waging war on the Pandavas. I can get you their kingdom and wealth without any bloodshed!' Duryodhana's eyes blazed with hope at these words.

'I am a master at the game of dice,' continued Sakuni. 'Yudhishthira loves to play but is no match for me. Let us invite him for a game. As a kshatriya he will not refuse the challenge. Then see how I strip him of everything he owns. But first, we must get your father's permission. Yudhishthira will be unable to refuse an invitation from him.'

# 7. Ill-fated Game of Dice

'You have no reason to be unhappy, my child,' Dhritarashtra fondly addressed Duryodhana. 'You have power, prestige, wealth; you are the heir to my throne.' And then in a rare burst of fair-mindedness, he said, 'Why be jealous of your blameless cousins? They do not envy you. Learn to be content.'

'Contentment is the goal of fools, not kshatriyas,' Duryodhana stormed at his father. 'I cannot bear to see the prosperity of the Pandavas. I must wrest it from them or die trying.'

As always, weak-willed Dhritarashtra could not oppose his fiery son and assented to the game of dice. Brushing aside wise Vidura's warning that the game would only result in discord and enmity, he asked Vidura to invite Yudhishthira to Hastinapur on his behalf.

Yudhishthira knew fully well what the evil game could lead to, but he could not refuse his uncle's invitation, being bound by kshatriya honor. The Pandavas, Kunti, and Draupadi accompanied Vidura to Hastinapur with heavy hearts.

A magnificent hall had been erected for the game of dice. In the presence of King Dhritarashtra, the patriarch Bhishma, Acharya Drona, Acharya Kripa, Vidura, and other members of the court, the opponents took their places opposite one another. Yudhishthira and his brothers faced Duryodhana and a few of his brothers, Karna, and Sakuni.

'Gambling is not proper for kshatriyas,' Yudhishtira said. 'Why seek to defeat another by devious means?'

'It is a game of skill like any other,' retorted Sakuni. 'But if you are afraid to play, why not say no?'

'I am not afraid,' said Yudhishthira. 'We will play.'

Duryodhana was thrilled that finally, he could strip the Pandavas of their wealth and fame. 'My uncle Sakuni will cast the dice on my behalf,' he announced.

Yudhishthira hesitated since Sakuni was an unscrupulous gambler. 'It is not customary to gamble by proxy,' he said.

'Another excuse not to play?' sneered Sakuni.

'No,' said Yudhishtira. 'Play for Duryodhana if he insists.'

They began the fateful game.

'I stake all my priceless pearls,' Yudhishthira said and played his dice.

'I stake as many,' said Duryodhana and Sakuni threw down his dice.

'We win!' he cried.

'I stake all the gold in my treasury,' said Yudhishthira and played again.

'My wealth against yours,' said Duryodhana. 'Uncle, play!'

Sakuni threw down his dice. 'Duryodhana, we win again!' he exclaimed.

Yudhishthira staked thousands of richly-bedecked chariots, gold-girdled elephants, moon-white horses, a vast retinue of slaves, soldiers, cattle, all his wealth, his entire kingdom—and he lost everything. Even then, spurred by a strange madness, he played on. When there were no material possessions left to gamble away, he staked his brothers and then himself.

Having won their wealth, their kingdom, and the Pandavas themselves, Sakuni said, 'Yudhishthira you have one last chance to redeem your fortune. Stake Draupadi, your wife.'

Dismay and confusion swept the assembly at such profanity. Each individual wondered if the noble Yudhishthira would stoop so low.

'Yes, I stake her,' said Yudhishthira. His voice trembled, but he went on. 'Beautiful, slender-waisted, beloved Draupadi,' and he threw down his dice.

So did Sakuni, and the high hall rang with his triumphant roar, 'We win! Draupadi is ours!'

'Go Vidura,' commanded Duryodhana. 'Fetch the beautiful wife of the Pandavas. Henceforth she will sweep our rooms like our other slaves.'

Bhishma and Drona froze with horror. But Vidura's eyes flashed fire. 'You fool!' he hissed at his nephew. 'Can you not see what you are doing? Your rashness and barbarity will doom us all.'

He turned to the silent assembly. 'Yudhishthira had no right to stake Draupadi,' he said. 'Because by that time, he was no longer a free man with any rights of his own.'

'You work for us and swear by the Pandavas. Be careful of what you utter!' Hotheaded Duryodhana rebuked Vidura and sent a servant to bring Draupadi.

As the terrified servant narrated the shocking incident of how Yudhishthira had staked and lost everything, including his brothers, himself and finally his wife, Draupadi listened in growing disbelief and anger.

'Go to him that staked me,' she said bitterly, 'and ask him in front of the entire assembly whether he lost himself first or me.'

The servant did as directed, but Yudhishthira gave no reply to this stinging question.

'How dare she refuse to come? Go, drag her here!' Duryodhana ordered Dussasana, his younger brother. Just as an animal mauls its prey, the evil-minded Dussasana dragged Draupadi by her hair into the assembly hall.

At this horrifying sight, a groan of anguish burst from Bhima's heart. 'Who should I blame for this calamity but you?' he reprimanded Yudhishthira, who sat with his head bowed down in grief. 'Let me set fire to the hands that staked an innocent woman.'

'Control your anger,' Arjuna admonished Bhima. 'He gambled of his own free will and lost us all. But he is still our dear and elder brother. Do not let adversity, even as vile as this, divide us.'

With a great effort, Bhima controlled his anger. However, the torture continued.

'These once-great Pandavas are now Sakuni's slaves,' declared Karna. 'They have lost everything, even the garments on their bodies. So has their haughty queen. Strip her, Dussasana!'

With fiendish pleasure, Dussasana caught hold of Draupadi's garment in an attempt to disrobe her. The Kauravas egged him on and relished the evil deed, whereas the rest of the assembly shuddered and averted their eyes. But not even a single soul came to Draupadi's aid.

In utter desperation, she prayed to the Almighty for help, her only hope in this unspeakable torment. 'Save me, Lord of the Universe,' she pleaded, pouring her entire being into her prayers. 'Save me.'

As she prayed, the fabric of her garment grew longer and longer. Dussasana kept on pulling at it, but it continued to grow so that no matter how much he disrobed her, she remained modestly covered.

Finally, Dussasana was exhausted.

He sat down with the realization that he would never succeed since Draupadi's prayer had been answered.

'I will kill you, Dussasana!' shouted Bhima. 'I will kill you in battle with my bare hands and drink your blood!'

As Bhima uttered this terrible oath—flames crackled around his body like a burning tree, jackals howled, birds shrieked, and other signs of disaster darkened the palace.

The blind king who had till then rejoiced in the ill-gotten gains of his son, now felt threatened. He begged Draupadi to forgive his sons and returned to Yudhishthira all that he had lost.

Still dazed by the twists and turns of fate but infinitely relieved, the Pandavas left for Indraprastha.

# 8. Pandavas in Exile

Duryodhana was enraged at what his father had done. He refused to accept defeat. 'The Pandavas will never forgive us for insulting Draupadi,' he said. 'By returning their kingdom, you have made them even

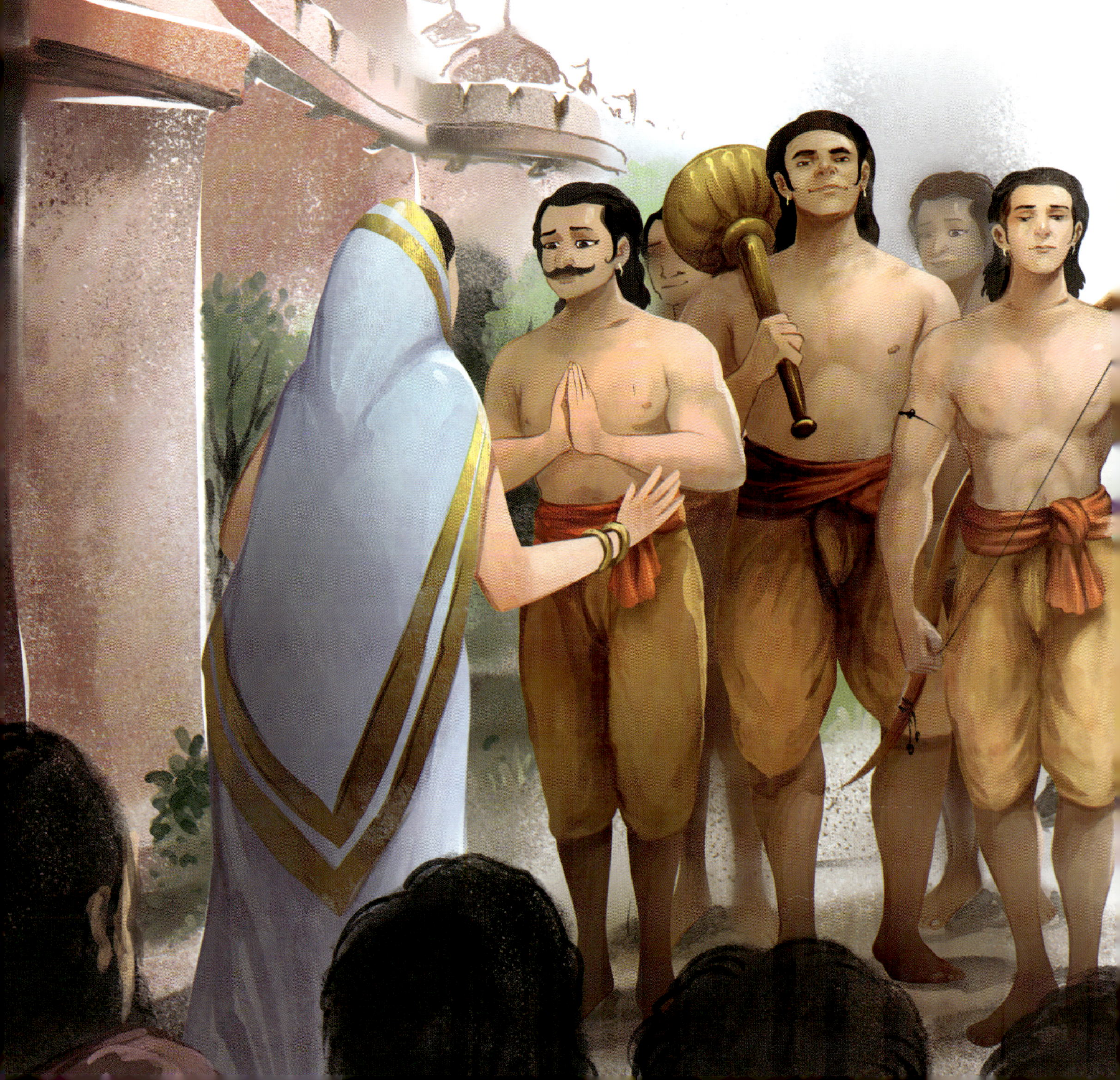

more dangerous. But there is a way out. Call them back for one more game and whoever loses this time goes to the forest for twelve years, with an additional year living in disguise. If exposed, the penalty gets reimposed for another thirteen years.'

'Father, do not hesitate. We will surely win the game, and by the time the Pandavas return to ask for their kingdom, we will be strong enough to tackle them.'

Against the wishes of the elders of the court, Dhritarashtra sent for Yudhishthira once again.

'I bow to fate,' said the eldest Pandava. Once again, he played against the treacherous Sakuni, and once again, he lost. But this time, there was no reprieve. Leaving their weeping mother Kunti in the care of Vidura, the five Pandavas and Draupadi took leave of the elders of Hastinapur. Many mourned their departure and followed them with tears and lamentation till Yudhishthira urged them to return to their homes. Lightning flashed across a cloudless sky, and the earth trembled at the injustice done to the sons of Pandu.

Meanwhile, the celestial sage Narada appeared before Dhritarashtra. 'Take heed, O King,' he said. 'Fourteen years from now, you will be childless. All your sons will die because of their avarice and wrong-doing.'

Anxiety gripped the sightless king. Blinded not only by fate but also by love for his firstborn son, there was little he could do to avert the approaching devastation.

The Pandavas crossed the Ganga and the Yamuna rivers and reached the Kamyaka forest. Krishna was defending his kingdom against invaders when he heard the news of the game of dice. He immediately hurried to the forest, accompanied by Draupadi's brother Drishtadumnya and many other fierce warriors.

Draupadi's tears fell uncontrollably before Krishna. Convulsed by grief and anger, she relived the agony inflicted upon her by Duryodhana and his companions.

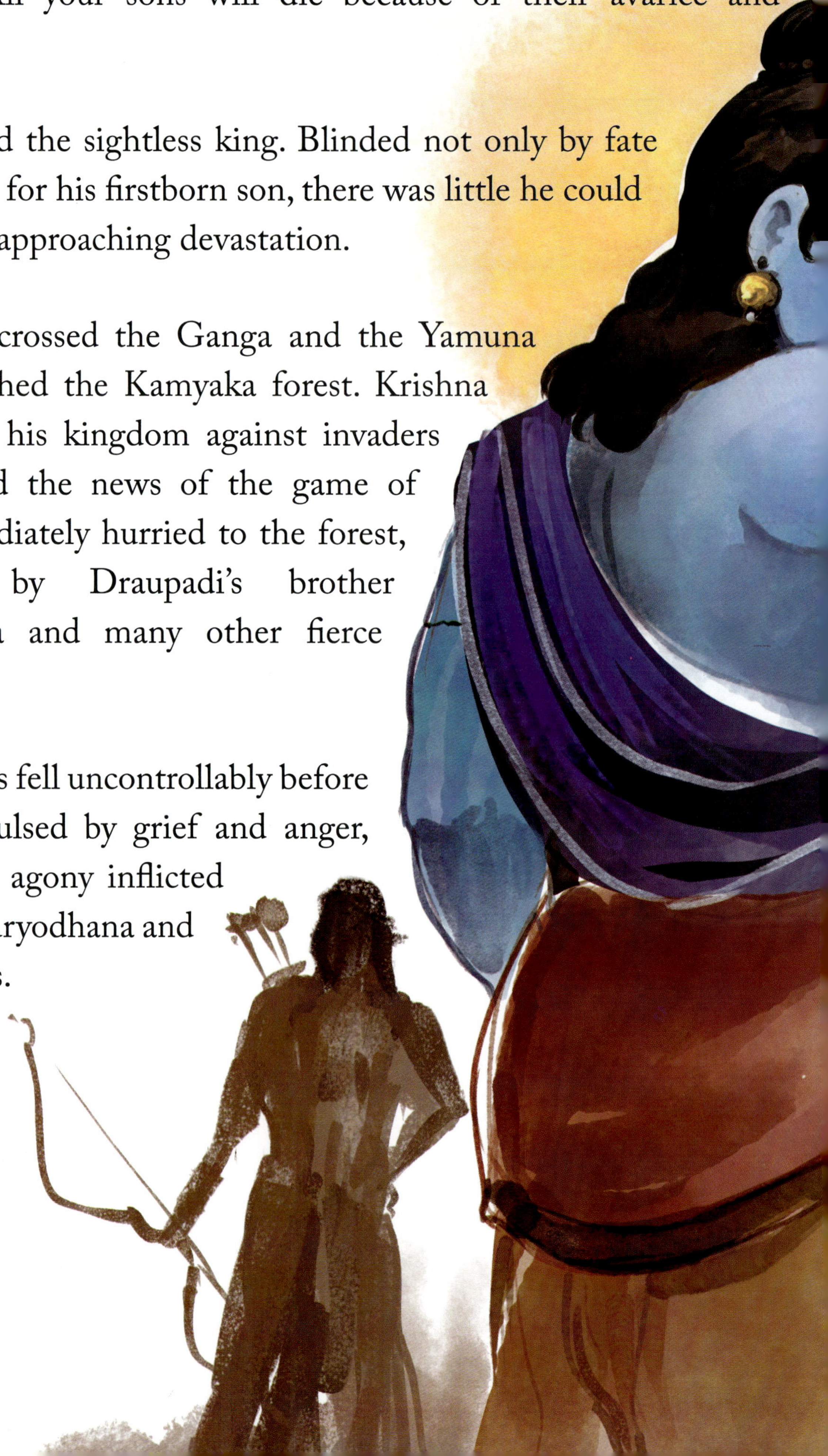

'Wipe your tears,' Krishna said gently. 'Each one that reviled you will die a bloody death on the battlefield. Their mothers and wives will weep over their corpses as you weep now over your shame. I vow to you Draupadi—all your wrongs will be avenged.'

Soon after Krishna's visit, the Pandavas moved to Dwaitavana, a forest peopled by many venerable sages. Their wise words soothed Yudhishthira's wounded soul, and he spent many peaceful, happy hours in their company. However, the other Pandavas and Draupadi were not so patient. Together they urged Yudhishthira to fight and win back their kingdom. They suggested that he disregard the unfair penalty imposed by the Kauravas.

Being the son of Dharma and the embodiment of patience and righteousness, Yudhishthira blamed himself for the misery that the game of dice had brought upon his loved ones. But even for them, he would not go back on his word. He was deeply worried as he knew that

after their thirteen years of exile, war was inevitable. Duryodhana would never return their kingdom. He thought of the formidable warriors who would fight beside Duryodhana due to their allegiance to the throne of Hastinapur—the indomitable Bhishma, Acharya Drona, Acharya Kripa, and Karna, the supreme archer. He wondered how the Pandavas would confront such peerless heroes?

Soon after, Rishi Vyasa visited Yudhishthira and his brothers in the forest. He advised Yudhishthira to send Arjuna to acquire the celestial weapons once promised to him by his father, Lord Indra. Yudhishthira agreed, and Arjuna ventured on a long and arduous journey.

His brothers waited for him anxiously. Many months passed before Arjuna returned, successful. Armed with Lord Shiva's deadly weapon Pasupati, the divine weapons given to him by his father Indra, and the celestial Gandiva bow that he had already obtained from Varuna, Lord of the Seas, Arjuna was now truly invincible.

During the exile, several brahmins visited the Pandavas in the forest. One of them then went to Hastinapur and told Dhritarashtra of their poverty and hardships as forest dwellers. The old king was stricken with guilt and remorse, but Duryodhana was exultant. He wished to see his cousins and flaunt his wealth before them.

Duryodhana entered the forest with a large retinue and attempted to set up camp near a beautiful lake, close to the Pandavas' home. However, several gandharvas, the celestial minstrels already living there, resisted the might of Duryodhana's army, defeated the Kauravas, and took Duryodhana prisoner.

'The gandharvas have done our work for us!' Bhima announced with delight.

But Yudhishthira upbraided him. 'This is not the time for settling scores,' he said. 'Do not forget Duryodhana is our brother, and he needs our help. You must rescue him from the gandharvas.'

Very unwilling yet obedient, Arjuna and Bhima freed Duryodhana from the gandharvas. The proud prince returned to Hastinapur, humbled before those he had sought to humiliate.

The twelfth year of exile was almost over. One day, when the brothers had gone deep into the forest, Yudhishthira asked Nakula to locate a source of drinking water. When Nakula did not return for a long time, Yudhishthira sent Sahadeva to look for him. He, too, did not return. Yudhishthira sent Arjuna, then Bhima, but no one returned. Very worried by their disappearance, he set out in search of his brothers and found them lying lifeless beside a pool of clear water.

Yudhishthira broke down and wept. His tears drenched the peaceful faces of Bhima, Arjuna, Nakula and Sahadeva. There were no marks of injury on their bodies. How had they died? Was the water poisoned? Beset by sorrow and thirst, Yudhishthira went to the water's edge to drink.

'Stop!' cried a voice. 'You cannot drink before answering my questions. Your brothers disobeyed me, and they died. This lake is mine.'

Yudhishthira realized it must be a yaksha, a demi-god. 'Ask your questions,' he said humbly. 'I will answer to the best of my ability.'

'What is happiness?' asked the yaksha.

'Happiness is the result of good conduct,' replied Yudhishthira.

'Which loss yields joy instead of sorrow?'

'The loss of anger,' said Yudhishthira.

'What should a man give up to be wealthy?'

'Getting rid of desires makes a man wealthy,' Yudhishthira answered.

The yaksha asked Yudhishthira many deep and searching questions. Yudhishthira answered them all carefully and wisely. Immensely pleased with Yudhishthira, the yaksha granted him a boon by which one of his brothers could come back to life. Yudhishthira asked for Nakula to be revived.

The yaksha was intrigued by Yudhishthira's response. 'Why Nakula?' he asked. 'Strong-armed Bhima or the invincible bowman Arjuna would be of greater use to you.'

'My father had two wives, Kunti and Madri,' said Yudhishthira. 'I, one of Kunti's sons, survive. It is only fair that the other survivor should be one of Madri's sons.'

'My son, I was only testing you. Your nobility and wisdom will win you eternal renown,' said the yaksha, who was really Dharmaraja, the god of righteousness, Yudhishthira's father. Assuming his true form, he embraced his son and brought the four other Pandavas back to life.

'Your sufferings will soon end,' he said. 'Courageously follow the path of dharma, and rest assured, victory will be yours.'

# 9. Pandavas in Matsya

Twelve years of the Pandavas' exile were over. But the hardest part was yet to come. They had to spend the thirteenth year in disguise, and if recognized, they would have to suffer another thirteen years of exile. It was what Duryodhana wanted. Thus, he sent his spies far and wide to discover where the Pandavas were hiding.

Yudhishthira and his brothers had decided to seek refuge in the prosperous kingdom of Matsya. King Virata, a mature and virtuous monarch, neither loyal nor subservient to the Kauravas, ruled Matsya. The Pandavas disguised themselves, carefully concealed their weapons, and sought employment at the court of King Virata.

There, Yudhishthira posed as a courtier, a brahmin well–versed in the game of dice which King Virata loved to play. Bhima, with his huge appetite, sought employment as a cook in the palace kitchen. Nakula and Sahadeva volunteered to look after the king's horses and cattle. Arjuna, disguised as a eunuch, offered to educate Virata's daughter Princess Uttara, in the fine arts of singing, dancing, and playing musical instruments. Arjuna had been taught these skills during his visit to heaven to gain mastery of celestial weapons, for this very eventuality. Draupadi offered her services as companion and attendant to King Virata's queen Sudeshna.

King Virata employed the five brothers and their queen, oblivious of their identities. Time passed, and they settled into their lowly duties, snatching a few moments whenever they could, with one another and waiting stoically for the year to end.

Meanwhile, Duryodhana was growing frantic as his spies had not been able to locate the Pandavas anywhere. When only a few weeks were left, he heard that the mighty commander-in-chief of King Virata's army had died in single combat on account of his trying to molest a woman. The killer of the commander-in-chief was no one else but Bhima, who had secretly come to the rescue of Draupadi.

Suspecting this, Duryodhana decided to invade the prosperous Matsya kingdom. If the Pandavas were hiding there, they would surely come to King Virata's aid. They would then be discovered and forced to go back into exile for another thirteen years.

Accordingly, Duryodhana's ally King Susarma attacked the Matsya kingdom from the south. King Virata rode out with his army to repulse the attack. All the Pandavas, except Arjuna, donned armor and fought for King Virata. Their bravery and skill in warfare tilted the scales of victory in Virata's favor.

But while the battle was still raging, Duryodhana invaded the Matsya kingdom from the north with a massive army and rounded up sixty thousand heads of cattle belonging to the king.

The cowherds came crying to Prince Uttara Kumara, telling him their plight as he was the only warrior left in the palace. 'Have no fear!' he declared grandly. 'I will fight the Kaurava army single-handed and recover our cattle. I am no less a warrior than the great Pandava Arjuna!'

'Take my eunuch as your charioteer,' Princess Uttara said to her brother. 'He has been charioteer to Arjuna. He will serve you well.'

Guided by the expert hands of the disguised Arjuna, Prince Uttara Kumara's chariot raced out of the palace gates to confront the great Kaurava army. The prince was no coward. But seeing the formidable warriors who led the army, Bhishma, Drona, Aswatthama, Duryodhana and Karna, his courage deserted him and he turned to flee.

'Take heart, my prince,' said Arjuna. 'You have nothing to fear.' He revealed his identity to the terrified youth. Then retrieving the weapons of the Pandavas from their place of concealment and twanging the mighty Gandiva bow, he announced his arrival on the battlefield.

'Arjuna has revealed himself before the stipulated period,' Duryodhana said to his grandfather Bhishma. 'The Pandavas must now endure another thirteen years of exile.'

'Your calculations are wrong,' said the venerable patriarch. 'The thirteenth year of exile is over. Now it is time to make peace with your cousins and give them their due.'

'Grandfather, I will give them nothing,' said Duryodhana. 'This talk of peace is intolerable. Let us end it and prepare for war.'

With Prince Uttara Kumara as his charioteer, Arjuna thundered into battle. His first arrows struck the ground at the feet of Bhishma and Drona, saluting the two beloved elders. Then he unleashed the power of the Gandiva. Like shafts of lightning, his arrows cut through the splendid Kaurava army and scattered it. So fierce was Arjuna's onslaught that no warrior could face him.

The Kaurava army was left dumbfounded as Arjuna recovered the stolen cattle and returned to the palace with the jubilant prince.

# 10. War is Inevitable

Now that the thirteenth year of exile was over, the Pandavas revealed their identity to King Virata. He was both amazed and delighted. To cement their friendship, he offered his daughter Princess Uttara's hand in marriage to Arjuna.

'I have looked upon her as a daughter,' said Arjuna. 'And so I accept her not for myself, but for my son Abhimanyu.'

Many illustrious kings, loyal to the Pandavas, attended the marriage of Abhimanyu and Uttara. Krishna was also there to bless them. So was Draupadi's father Dhrupada, ruler of Panchala.

After the joyful wedding ceremony, the assembled kings discussed the future course of action for the Pandavas. They decided to send Dhrupada's chief priest, a man of great wisdom, tact and learning, to Hastinapur as the Pandavas' emissary. He would counsel Dhritarashtra to follow the path of dharma and return to the Pandavas, the kingdom that the Kauravas unfairly took from them thirteen years ago.

At the same time, they were well aware of Duryodhana's greed, hostility, and influence over his father. So, they did not expect a peaceful settlement. The Pandavas had endured enough, and there was a limit to their endurance. War seemed inevitable.

While sending their messenger to Hastinapur to negotiate a peace treaty, the Pandavas started preparing for war. In Hastinapur, the Kauravas did the same.

Both the parties wished for the support of Sri Krishna. Therefore, both Arjuna and Duryodhana reached the city of Dwarka. When they arrived, Krishna was asleep. Duryodhana arrogantly seated himself near the head of the bed while Arjuna remained standing, with folded hands, near Krishna's feet. Krishna opened his eyes, saw Arjuna, and welcomed him. Then he turned and welcomed Duryodhana.

'I arrived here before Arjuna,' said Duryodhana. 'So you should honor my request and become my ally.'

'You may have reached here first, but my eyes first fell on Arjuna,' said Krishna. 'Also, he is younger than you. Tradition demands I give him preference. If there is a war, I will not fight in it. Arjuna, the choice is between my vast and powerful army and me, without any weapons. Whom do you choose?'

Arjuna fell at Krishna's feet with tears of devotion. 'I choose you, my lord,' he said. 'Only you.'

'Then the army is mine!' declared Duryodhana. 'I thank you, Krishna.' He left the palace jubilantly.

Krishna smiled. 'You made a foolish decision, Arjuna,' he gently said, 'choosing me instead of my army.'

'My lord, you mock me,' Arjuna said humbly. 'With you as my charioteer, I can conquer the world! All the armies of the world are nothing before your glory.'

As decided, King Dhrupada's chief priest reached Hastinapur and pleaded the cause of justice before the court. Bhishma and Vidura agreed with him, but Duryodhana and his supporters were against any fair settlement. The indecisive king Dhritarashtra decided to send his answer to Yudhishthira through his messenger Sanjaya.

'Let us avoid the evil of war at any cost,' was the message. 'You are righteous men. Do not swerve from the path of dharma even if my foolish sons refuse to return your kingdom. Remain patient and strive for peace.'

Yudhishthira was sorely disappointed by this partisan reply to his plea for justice. Yet he persevered. 'Go tell our kinsmen,' he said to Sanjaya, 'we do not desire war even though we have been insulted and treated unjustly. We do not even ask for our entire kingdom. Give us only five villages, and we will be content.'

Even though Yudhishthira knew that Duryodhana would not part with even this much territory, he wondered whether a war was the only solution. In his anguish, he turned to Krishna, who always guided the Pandavas in times of perplexity and distress.

'Virtuous prince,' Krishna said to Yudhishthira, 'You have done more than your duty, but the Kauravas seem bent on destroying themselves. I will go and counsel Dhritarashtra to restrain his sons. Let us make one last attempt to avert calamity.'

Hastinapur accorded Krishna a warm welcome. All eyes were on him as he addressed Dhritarashtra and reminded him of his duty to his nephews.

'Treat them fairly. Return their kingdom and let there be peace,' he said. 'It does not behoove a king of the great Kuru dynasty to neglect justice and invite the horrors of war.'

Dhritarashtra, Gandhari, Bhishma, Vidura, and Drona, all agreed with Krishna. But none could sway Duryodhana from his chosen path of action.

'Yudhishthira staked his kingdom and lost it. Why does he beg for it now? If I had my way, I would not have given them anything. The entire kingdom is mine, and I will not part with the tiniest fraction of it. Let there be war. We will win or die trying.'

There was nothing left for anyone to say. Duryodhana had already made up his mind. In his foolishness, Duryodhana attempted to imprison Krishna before he could persuade the assembly against war. The Lord of the Universe smiled as Duryodhana's soldiers rushed towards him. For a blinding instant, he revealed himself in all his divinity. The next moment the stunned court was empty of his dazzling presence.

# 11. Noble Karna's Sacrifice

Before leaving Hastinapur, Krishna took Karna to a place outside the city where they could be alone.

'Karna,' said Krishna, 'you are not only a great warrior but also a learned man, well versed in the holy Vedas. Why do you champion the cause of a man as unworthy as Duryodhana?'

'My lord, I know Duryodhana for what he is,' said Karna. 'But I am bound by ties of love and loyalty. Duryodhana is the only man who did not care that I am a sutaputra. He accepted me and loved me for who I am, and I would do the same for him even though I realize the path he is pursuing will destroy us as well as many of the finest warriors of this world.'

'Noble Karna, it is time you knew the truth,' said Krishna. 'You are not a sutaputra. You are not the son of Adiratha and Radha.'

'Time and again, I have felt this but remained unaware of the truth. Who am I, then, my lord, who am I?' Karna's voice throbbed with a lifetime of yearning for the unattainable.

'You are the eldest son of a noble queen. You have five brothers, unequaled in this world in valor and virtue. The Pandavas are your brothers, Kunti is your mother, and Surya, the Sun God is your father. Kunti bore you when she was still a maiden. Karna, listen to me carefully. You should join your brothers. They will welcome you with open arms, and in the eyes of the world, you will be the eldest son of King Pandu. Everything they own will be yours to command.'

'It is too late now, my lord,' said Karna. 'If Queen Kunti is my mother, then I am the son she cast away and never claimed. It is Radha's love that has sustained me all these years. She is the only mother, and Duryodhana is the only brother that I know. How can I abandon him, especially now when he needs me the most?'

Krishna's eyes were full of compassion. 'Noble soul, I wished to save you from death,' he said. 'Death does not frighten me, my lord,' said Karna. 'It will end this life of pain and longing. Please promise me that you will not disclose the secret of my birth to my brothers. As my younger brother, Yudhishthira would give me the kingdom were he to win it. And I would give it to Duryodhana. My lord, leave me to my fate. The only happiness I wish for is a good name. I hope to die with honor on the battlefield.'

There were tears in their eyes as they embraced. With a heavy heart, Krishna returned to the Pandavas. The failure of Krishna's peace mission meant only one thing. War was inevitable.

Even before Krishna's mission, it was obvious that a clash between Karna and Arjuna was certain. Troubled by this, Arjuna's father, Indra Deva, devised a plan to weaken Karna.

Karna was well-known for his generosity. Every morning after his prayers, he donated to the needy, whatever was asked of him.

Indra took advantage of this large heartedness. Disguised as a brahmin, he appeared before Karna and asked him for his golden armor and earrings, which protected Karna from all weapons.

Although Surya, the Sun God had forewarned him of Indra's trickery, Karna did not hesitate. He gave the brahmin what he asked for. Indra was humbled by Karna's generosity and courage.

In return, he gave Karna the mighty Shakti weapon to be used just once. Then he disappeared.

Tormented by anxiety for the welfare of her sons, Kunti sought out her firstborn, Karna, whom she perceived as the most dangerous enemy of the Pandavas. She went to the bank of the river Ganga where Karna was deep in meditation. Kunti waited till he finished his prayers. Then she spoke, revealing to him that she was his mother and urged him to abandon Duryodhana and join his brothers. It seemed to Karna that the Sun God, his father, whom he had always worshipped, echoed Kunti's appeal.

Karna steeled his heart. 'Great queen, if I were to break faith with the Kauravas, I would be the basest of men,' he said. 'I am their anchor, and they rely upon me greatly. I cannot abandon them, but I also cannot let you go away disappointed. I know you came to ask me for the lives of your sons. Indra Deva, Lord of the Heavens, came to me too, disguised as a brahmin. He asked me for my kavacha and kundala—my impregnable armor and earrings—to ensure the victory of his son Arjuna. I did not refuse him, nor can I refuse you. I promise not to harm Yudhishthira, Bhima, Nakula, and Sahadeva. It is only Arjuna that I will fight to the bitter end, be it his or mine. And so, when all this is over, you will still have five sons. That much I can promise.'

Kunti trembled as she embraced her valiant, generous-hearted, firstborn son. Her tears fell on his bowed head, and she left in silence.

Both sides marshaled their forces and marched towards the battlefield of Kurukshetra. The fiery prince Drishtadumnya was appointed commander-in-chief of the Pandava army. The ancient yet peerless warrior Bhishma led the Kaurava forces.

'I am bound to the throne of Hastinapur,' Bhishma said to Duryodhana. 'So I will fight to the best of my abilities. Each day I will kill thousands of your enemies. However, I will not harm the Pandavas since they are as dear to me as you are.'

Apprehensive and frightened, Dhritarashtra sat alone in his palace. Sage Vyasa, his father, came to him. 'The iniquity of your sons has doomed Hastinapur and will stain the illustrious throne of your ancestors with blood. Inauspicious omens forecast a great massacre, the likes of which this world has never known. If you wish, I can grant you the vision to see it.'

'No, revered one,' said Dhritarashtra. 'Who would wish to see the death of his own flesh and blood? Let me remain blind, but if I could have news of the war...'

'You will, my son,' said Vyasa. 'I will endow

your charioteer Sanjaya with special powers. His eyes and ears will miss nothing, and he will narrate to you faithfully what transpires on the battlefield.'

Before the beginning of the war, the fearless warriors of both sides pledged to honor the traditional rules of warfare. Soldiers would only fight those similarly armed. The ones who were disarmed, panicked, or surrendered, would not be harmed. Neither would charioteers, supply-carrying groups, drummers, or conch-blowers.

The battle was about to start. Suits of armor glittered in the morning sun like countless gems as the two great armies confronted each other on the plains of Kurukshetra. On horseback, on elephant back, in chariots, and on foot, thousands upon thousands of fine warriors stood face to face with their destiny.

In his shining chariot, driven by white horses, Arjuna took up the mighty Gandiva bow and addressed Krishna, his charioteer.

'My lord, set the chariot between the two armies,' he said. 'Friends and foes, let me view them all.'

Krishna drove the gleaming chariot into the middle of the battlefield.

Arjuna surveyed his kinsmen, teachers, old friends and companions, many of them now arrayed against him, ready to kill or be killed in battle. Pitamaha Bhishma, his beloved grandfather, Acharya Drona, his revered guru, stood before him like two majestic pillars that he knew he would have to shatter before he could bring down the house of the Kauravas.

Arjuna's heart filled with grief and pity. 'I cannot kill them, Krishna,' he said. 'They are my own people. The Kauravas may have wronged us but they are our brothers. I do not want a victory soaked in their blood. I will not fight this war.'

The great Gandiva slipped from his fingers as he sank back in the chariot.

‘This weakness is unworthy of you, great warrior,’ said Krishna. ‘Rise and take up your Gandiva. As a kshatriya, it is your duty to fight a righteous war. But fight with an even mind. Treat both victory and defeat, both pleasure and pain, alike. He, who fulfills his duty with no thought of reward; whose mind is steady and tranquil, he is the supreme yogi.’

‘Arjuna, you delude yourself when you grieve for those who are about to die. Death is only of the physical body. The atman, man’s real indwelling self is deathless. Weapons cannot kill it. So, do not grieve.’

‘Fix your mind on me. In age after age, whenever evil threatens to engulf the world, I come to protect the good and to establish dharma.’

‘Look upon me Arjuna, I grant you divine vision to see me as I truly am.’

Glowing like a million suns, infinitely beautiful, encompassing all creation, the Almighty Lord of the Universe revealed himself to Arjuna.

Then all was as it had been. And Krishna was once more his beloved friend, guide, and charioteer. Arjuna took up the Gandiva bow.

‘My lord, you have removed my doubts and given me peace,’ he said. ‘Great Krishna, I am ready. I will fight.’

# 12. Mighty Bhishma

In the lull before the storm and the silence that preceded the clamor of battle, both armies were amazed when Yudhishthira removed his armor, shed his weapons, and walked barefoot towards Bhishma. Yudhishthira's brothers hurried to question him, fearing that he was going to surrender. Thinking the same, the Kauravas rejoiced. Yudhishthira walked on, silent and resolute.

'He is going to seek the blessings of the elders before the start of war,' Krishna told Arjuna. 'It is the right and honorable thing to do.'

Yudhishthira bent low before Bhishma and touched his feet. His eyes were full of tears. 'Pitamaha,' he said, 'allow us to take up arms against you. We need your blessings.'

'My blessings are always with you.' Bhishma said lovingly while raising Yudhishthira up. 'I am bound to the throne of Hastinapur that has supported me ever since I renounced my claim to kingship. And so, in this cruel war, I find myself standing against you. Fight well, my child. Your cause is just.'

Yudhishthira then sought his gurus—Drona and Kripa. Like Bhishma, they greeted him with great affection and blessed him. Yudhishthira walked back to his army and donned his armor once again. As he did so, conches blew, heralding the start of the battle.

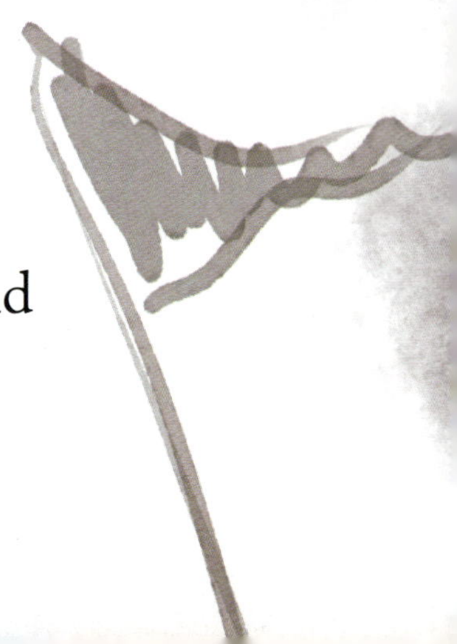

The earth trembled as the two great armies swept across the plain towards each other, meeting in a mighty tumult that shook the heavens. The field of Kurukshetra rang with the thunder of hoofs and chariot wheels, the twanging of bowstrings, the hissing of deadly arrows speeding through the air, the clash of sword against sword, the roars of fiery warriors, and the cries of the wounded and dying.

The tall majestic figure of Bhishma, clad in white on a silver chariot swept through the Pandava army like a hurricane. Accomplished warriors like Arjuna's son Abhimanyu were helpless before his fiery onslaught. By the end of the first day's battle, thousands had perished at Bhishma's hands. The young princes of Matsya, King Virata's sons—Uttara Kumara and Sveta—lay dead on the battlefield.

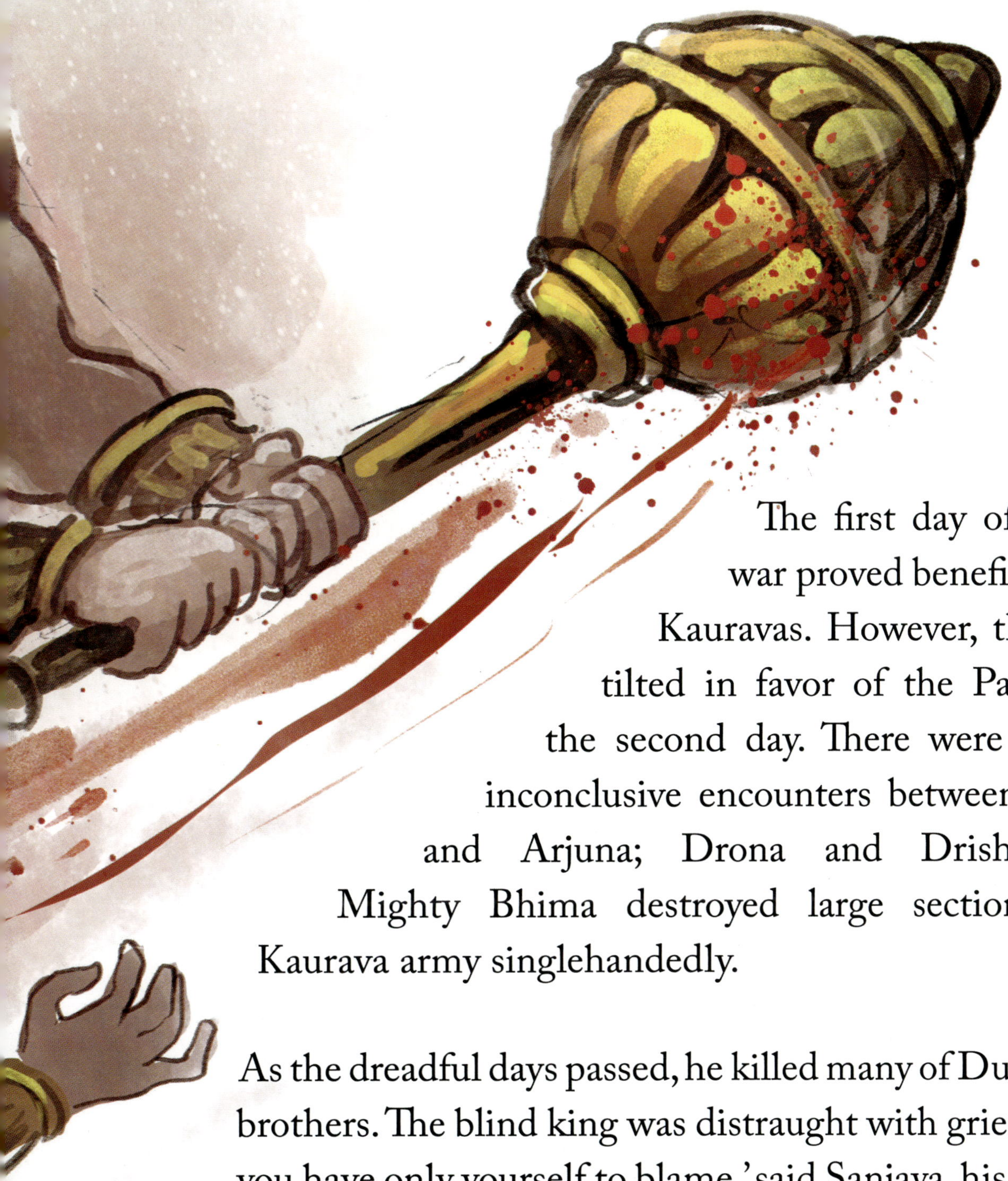

The first day of the great war proved beneficial for the Kauravas. However, the balance tilted in favor of the Pandavas on the second day. There were fierce but inconclusive encounters between Bhishma and Arjuna; Drona and Drishtadumnya. Mighty Bhima destroyed large sections of the Kaurava army singlehandedly.

As the dreadful days passed, he killed many of Duryodhana's brothers. The blind king was distraught with grief. 'My lord, you have only yourself to blame,' said Sanjaya, his charioteer, whose task was to narrate whatever happened on the battlefield to Dhritrashtra. 'You ignored the counsel of the great Krishna and the elders of the Kuru empire. You did nothing to restrain the greed of your sons and let injustice thrive. Now they are paying for their iniquity.'

On the evening of the fourth day, after the fighting was over, Duryodhana went to Bhishma's tent. 'Pitamaha,' he said, 'my army boasts of such unbeaten warriors as you, Acharya Drona, Acharya Kripa, and Aswatthama. You alone are enough to demolish the entire army of the Pandavas. Then why does victory elude me?'

'My son, victory eludes you because you have turned away from the righteous path,' said the patriarch. 'Even now, it is not too late to end this war. Do you not realize that your cousins are undefeatable? Krishna is with them, my child. He is the incarnation of Lord Vishnu, born in the world of men to redeem it from wrongdoing. Stop this terrible bloodshed. Make peace with the Pandavas.'

Silently Duryodhana took his leave. The whole night his thoughts kept him awake.

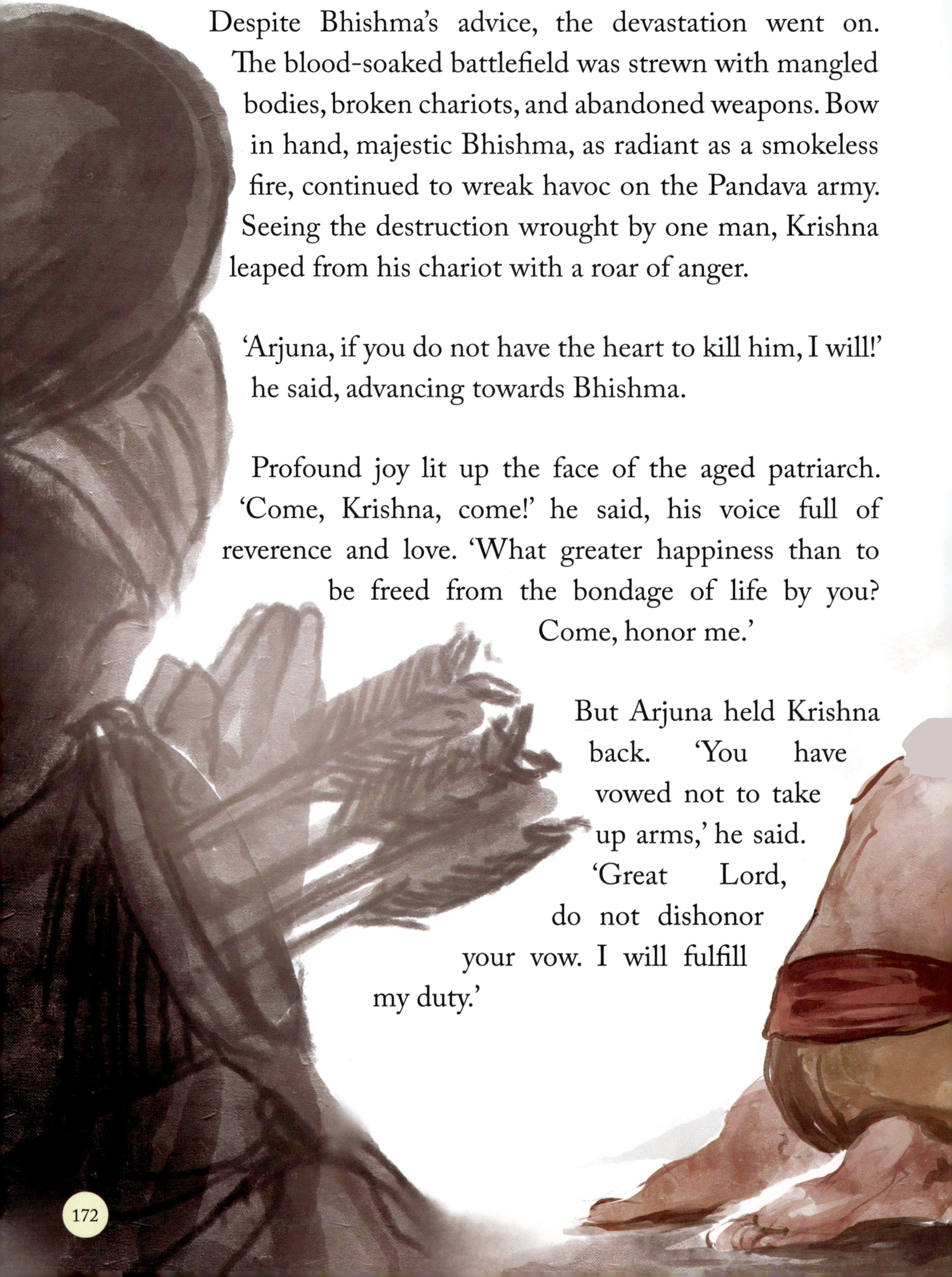

Despite Bhishma's advice, the devastation went on. The blood-soaked battlefield was strewn with mangled bodies, broken chariots, and abandoned weapons. Bow in hand, majestic Bhishma, as radiant as a smokeless fire, continued to wreak havoc on the Pandava army. Seeing the destruction wrought by one man, Krishna leaped from his chariot with a roar of anger.

'Arjuna, if you do not have the heart to kill him, I will!' he said, advancing towards Bhishma.

Profound joy lit up the face of the aged patriarch. 'Come, Krishna, come!' he said, his voice full of reverence and love. 'What greater happiness than to be freed from the bondage of life by you? Come, honor me.'

But Arjuna held Krishna back. 'You have vowed not to take up arms,' he said. 'Great Lord, do not dishonor your vow. I will fulfill my duty.'

On the evening of the ninth day of battle, the five Pandavas and Krishna went to meet Bhishma. The old man embraced them with great affection. Blinded by his tears and hardly able to speak, Yudhishthira said, 'Pitamaha, there is no other way. If this war is to end, we must kill you. We cannot win while you are alive.'

Bhishma stroked Yudhishthira's bent head lovingly. Many years ago, his father, King Santanu, had granted him the ability to choose the time of his death. He would die only when he wished to die. And he knew that time was approaching.

'You are right, my child,' he said. 'No one can kill me till I lay down my arms. And I will not fight a woman or a man who was once a woman. Tomorrow let Arjuna place Sikhandin in his chariot. When he attacks me, I will not fight back.'

The warrior Sikhandin was Princess Amba who had long ago vowed to kill Bhishma for ruining her life. Amba had been reborn as Sikhandin for that one purpose.

Arjuna rode straight towards the silver chariot on the tenth day of the battle. All the frantic efforts of the Kauravas to protect Bhishma were of no avail. Sikhandin's arrows pierced the patriarch's chest as he stood calm and defenseless. From behind Sikhandin, his heart breaking, Arjuna shot arrow after arrow at his beloved grandfather in whose lap he used to play as a child.

Bhishma fell from his silver chariot, his entire body pierced with arrows. The earth trembled as it received the wounded body of the noblest of men.

Fighting ceased, and the Kauravas and the Pandavas gathered around him. Bhishma lay on a bed of arrows. He asked for a pillow to support his head, and numerous soft pillows were quickly brought to him.

'Arjuna,' said Bhishma, 'give me a pillow that befits a warrior.'

The grief-stricken prince shot three powerful arrows into the ground for Bhishma to rest his head.

'This is good,' said Bhishma. 'I will remain alive until the sun begins his northward journey in the heavens. Leave me now, but before you go, I crave some water to drink.'

The choicest drinks were brought for him. But once again, Bhishma turned to Arjuna.

Arjuna raised the mighty Gandiva bow and shot an arrow into the earth near Bhishma's head. A jet of pure, cool water gushed out of the ground. The goddess Ganga had come to slake the thirst of her dying son.

'See Duryodhana, who else but Arjuna could

perform such a deed?' said Bhishma. 'Make peace with your cousins. Let my fall bring an end to this senseless carnage.'

# 13. Abhimanyu - The Brave Warrior

Karna had decided not to fight as long as Bhishma was the commander of the Kaurava army. There had always been hostility between the two. Aiding Duryodhana in his evil schemes against the Pandavas, Karna had repeatedly incurred Bhishma's wrath. He had always scorned the patriarch's pleas for peace and justice. But now, as the great warrior lay dying on his bed of arrows, Karna came to him at night and wept at his feet.

Affectionately, Bhishma welcomed him. 'Karna, I bear you no ill-will,' he said. 'Valiant one, you are oblivious of your own greatness. You are the eldest of the Pandavas, son of Queen Kunti, and the Sun God Surya. Befriend your brothers, and end this war. The Pandavas are undefeatable.'

'I know,' said Karna. 'And yet I must fight against my brothers and be true to Duryodhana. Give me the permission to do my duty. And forgive me if my unkind words have ever hurt you.'

Bhishma sighed. 'I had hoped that my end would bring peace,' he said. 'Alas! I have failed. Noble son of Kunti, my blessings are with you. Fight well, but fight without anger or hope of reward.'

Karna then went back to Duryodhana and advised him to appoint his acharya, the unconquerable warrior Drona, as the next commander of the Kaurava forces. Duryodhana asked Drona to capture Yudhishthira alive. He thought this would be the quickest way to end the war. Killing Yudhishthira would only invite the wrath of Arjuna and Krishna while a

captive Yudhishthira could be persuaded to play another game of dice. He would surely lose, earning for himself and his brothers another long period of exile. The acharya was disgusted by Duryodhana's ignoble reasoning but was relieved that he did not seek the death of the wise and gentle Pandava.

Drona took command of the Kaurava forces on the eleventh day of the war. Like a raging fire, he decimated the Pandava army wherever he went. Many fine warriors closely guarded Yudhishthira. Through their spies, the Pandavas had come to know of the plan to capture him alive. Drona cut through Yudhishthira's defenses and was on the point of seizing him when Arjuna's chariot appeared, coursing through a river of blood. Deadly arrows from the Gandiva darkened the sky and pushed Drona back from victory. He knew he was no match for his beloved former pupil.

The next day, on the twelfth day of battle, Duryodhana's ally King Susarma and his brothers took a solemn oath to challenge Arjuna and lure him, away from Yudhishthira, to the southern end of the battlefield where they would either kill him or perish in the attempt.

As a kshatriya, Arjuna could not ignore their challenge. He followed them to the southern end of the battlefield, where all day long, the Gandiva rained death on Susarma's army. Meanwhile, Drona made repeated attempts to capture Yudhishthira, killing many brave generals who barred his way. When evening came, he had still not been successful.

On the thirteenth day of the war, Drona followed a new strategy. While Susarma challenged Arjuna, once again, to battle in the far corner of the field, Drona arranged his army in the chakravyuha, a circular lotus-like formation. At the heart of the lotus stood Duryodhana, flanked by such expert warriors as Karna, Dussasana, Acharya Kripa, and Drona's son Aswatthama. In this formation, the Kaurava forces were invincible. They repulsed the Pandava attack time and again, inflicting heavy losses on the enemy.

Besides Arjuna and Krishna, who were far away, Arjuna's son Abhimanyu was the only warrior who knew how to penetrate the chakravyuha. He did not, however, know a way out in case the need arose. Seeing the plight of his soldiers and fearing defeat, Yudhishthira asked his nephew to break and enter the chakravyuha.

'We will be right behind you,' he said. 'You will not be alone and unprotected, even for a moment.'

Abhimanyu was Arjuna's son by his second wife Subhadra, Krishna's sister. He attacked the Kaurava formation with the power and grace of a young lion attacking a herd of elephants. As he forced his way through, Yudhishthira, Bhima, and a host of Pandava warriors were right behind him, only to have their way barred by Jayadratha, king of the Sindhus. Jayadratha had obtained a boon from the gods that once in his life, he would be able to defy the Pandavas single-handed, provided Krishna and Arjuna were not present. This was the moment. Powerless to oppose him, the Pandavas saw the chakravyuha close remorselessly around their brave nephew.

For a long time, Abhimanyu fought fearlessly, worsting Duryodhana, Karna, and many other experienced fighters in single combat. Like a rock that stands firm against the fury of the sea, he withstood their joint assault, although such warfare was against all norms of chivalry.

When Abhimanyu remained unbeaten, the Kaurava warriors cast aside all the rules of fair fighting laid down at the start of the war. They killed Abhimanyu's horses and charioteer, broke his bow and sword with sharp arrows, and pierced his shield.

Wounded, defenseless, surrounded by enemies, Abhimanyu picked up one of the wheels of his chariot. He whirled it like a discus and scattered his opponents. But they regrouped and shattered Abhimanyu's last weapon. Picking up a mace, he fought a desperate battle with Dussasana's son. Both fell to the ground. Dussasana's son rose first, and even as Abhimanyu was struggling to his feet, he hit him on the head with his mace and killed him.

Brave Abhimanyu died, murdered by his uncles and cousins, by his father's gurus, and by men he had revered as noble warriors. His murderers shouted with joy, and their triumphant roar pierced the hearts of Yudhishthira and his brothers.

Arjuna and Krishna returned at sunset after defeating King Susarma's army. They found the camp engulfed in silence and sorrow. When Arjuna heard how his beloved son had fallen, grief and anger overwhelmed him. He was inconsolable.

'Jayadratha sent my son to his death,' he said bitterly. 'It was he who pitted my child against an entire army. Before the sun sets tomorrow, I vow that I will kill this evil man or immolate myself if I fail.'

As Arjuna spoke, the twang of his mighty bow resounded over the battlefield and dismayed the rejoicing Kauravas. Their spies brought them news of the oath Arjuna had taken. The terrified Jayadratha asked Duryodhana's permission to leave the battle and return to his kingdom. But Duryodhana assured him of protection and prevailed upon him to remain.

# 14. 'Aswatthama is dead!'

On the fourteenth day of the war, the entire Kaurava army sought to protect Jayadratha. Fighting fiercely, Arjuna advanced towards his target. Yudhishthira sent Bhima to aid him. Karna intercepted Bhima, and the two formidable warriors clashed like angry

tigers. As Bhima gained the upper hand, Duryodhana sent several of his brothers to help Karna, and Bhima slew them all.

Arjuna neared Jayadratha. A frantic Duryodhana accused Drona of fighting half-heartedly against his favorite pupils, the Pandavas.

'This is war, Duryodhana,' the acharya said grimly. 'Wars are not as easily manipulated and won as games of dice. Be reassured. I am doing my best.'

The sun was about to set, and the battle between Arjuna and Jayadratha was still raging. Using his divine powers, Krishna covered the sun with darkness. The Kauravas thought the sun had set, saving Jayadratha. They shouted in triumph. As soon as they let their guard down and looked up at the sky, Krishna told Arjuna to shoot. A deadly arrow sped from the Gandiva and severed Jayadratha's head from his body. After which, the sun reappeared in the sky for a few shining moments before setting.

All the efforts of the Kauravas to save Jayadratha had been futile. Duryodhana mourned the dead. Too late he realized how many brave men had died to satisfy his greed and ambition. Contrary to the norms of warfare, the battle continued throughout the night, and thousands of torches cast an eerie light on the dreadful scene.

Bhima's eldest son was an asura named Ghatochkacha, whose mother Bhima had met and married in the forest after the Pandavas had escaped from Varnavata. The huge superhuman Ghatochkacha came to the aid of the Pandavas. He wrought such havoc on the Kaurava forces, that

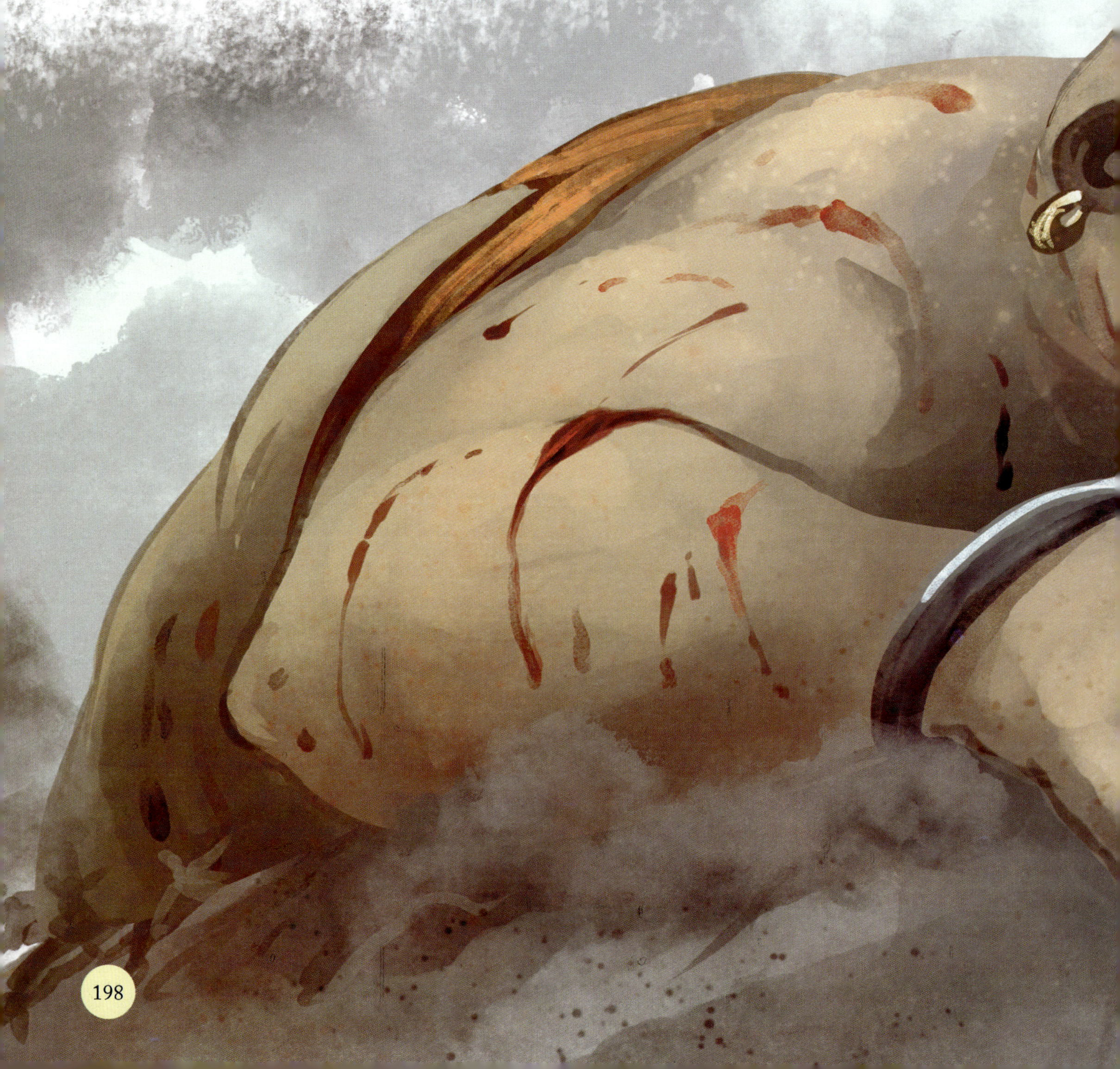

Karna was compelled to use the powerful Shakti weapon against him. This weapon was given to him by Lord Indra before the war in return for his impregnable armor. The Shakti could only be used once, and Karna had hoped to use it against Arjuna, in their final battle.

But duty decreed otherwise. Resigned to whatever fate had in store for him, Karna hurled the divine spear at Ghatochkacha, piecing the demon's chest. He fell headlong, crushing hundreds of soldiers beneath his lifeless body.

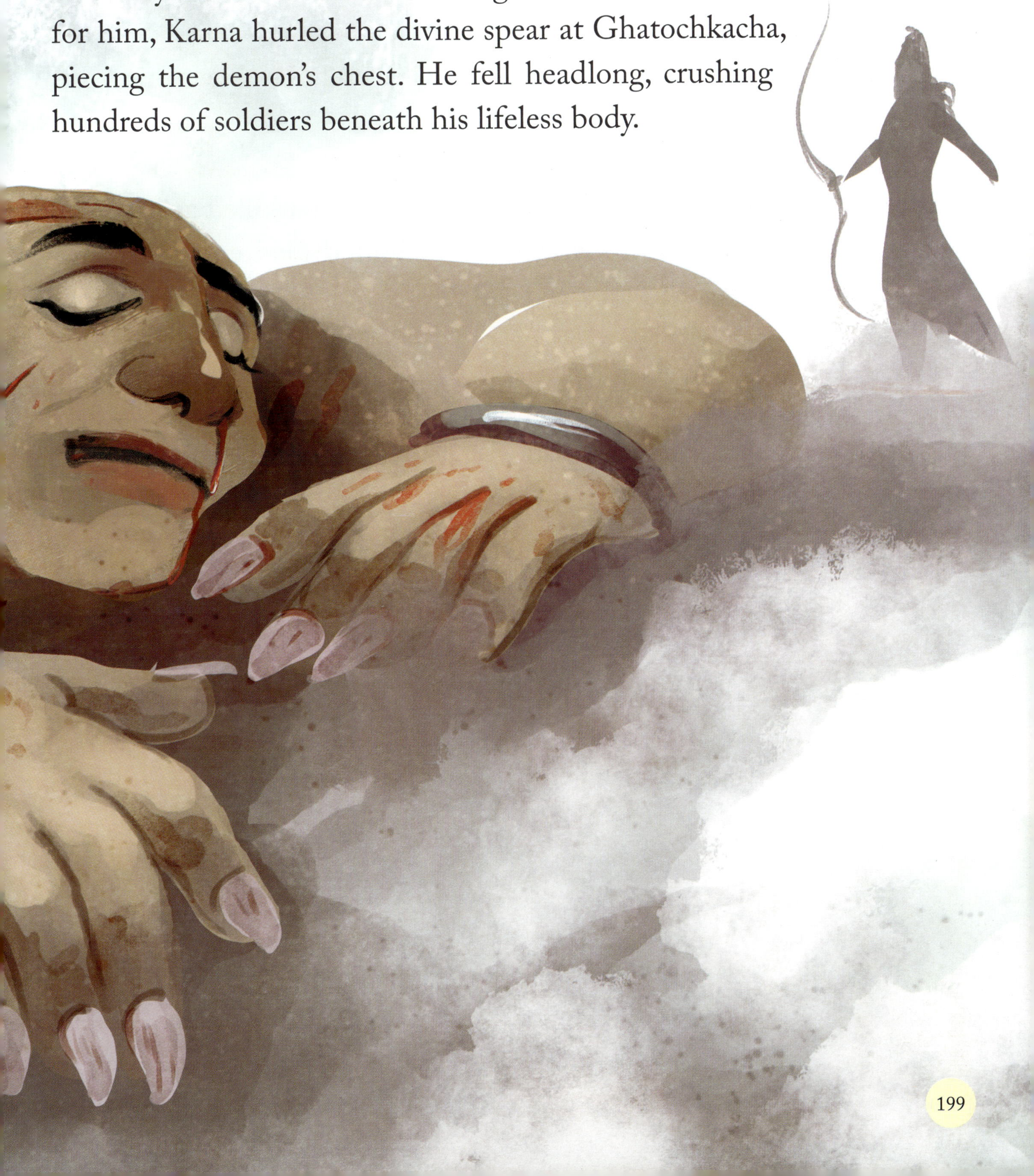

On the fifteenth day of battle, Drona fought like a man possessed. He mercilessly killed King Virata of Matsya and the Panchala king Dhrupada, his former friend and then enemy. Drona used divine weapons to massacre the soldiers of the Pandavas' army.

'We must stop him at all costs,' Krishna said to Arjuna. 'There is only one way. Announce that his son Aswatthama has been killed in battle. When he hears this terrible news, he will surely lay down his arms. Only then can he be defeated.'

Arjuna could not tell such a lie to his guru. Bhima killed an elephant named Aswatthama with his mace and shouted loud enough for the acharya to hear, 'Aswatthama is dead!'

The power drained from Drona's limbs but, suspecting a lie, he fought on. As he used another divine weapon to slaughter thousands of men and beasts, great rishis appeared in the sky to admonish him.

'Such fighting does not behoove a brahmin,' they said. 'Lay down your arms and return to the path of truth. Your life on earth is over.'

Disheartened and full of remorse, Drona turned to the only man he knew would never lie.

'Yudhishthira, is my son dead?' he asked.

The noble Pandava trembled as he told his first and last lie. 'Yes, Aswatthama is dead,' he said, adding under his breath, 'Aswatthama, the elephant.'

Till that moment, the wheels of Yudhishthira's chariot had remained a few inches above the ground. But now they touched the earth. Yudhishthira's lie had brought him down to the level of other men.

On hearing his son was dead. Drona abandoned his weapons and sat in meditation. Only Sanjaya, Krishna, Arjuna, and Yudhishthira saw Drona's spirit leave his body and ascend to the heavens in a glow of light.

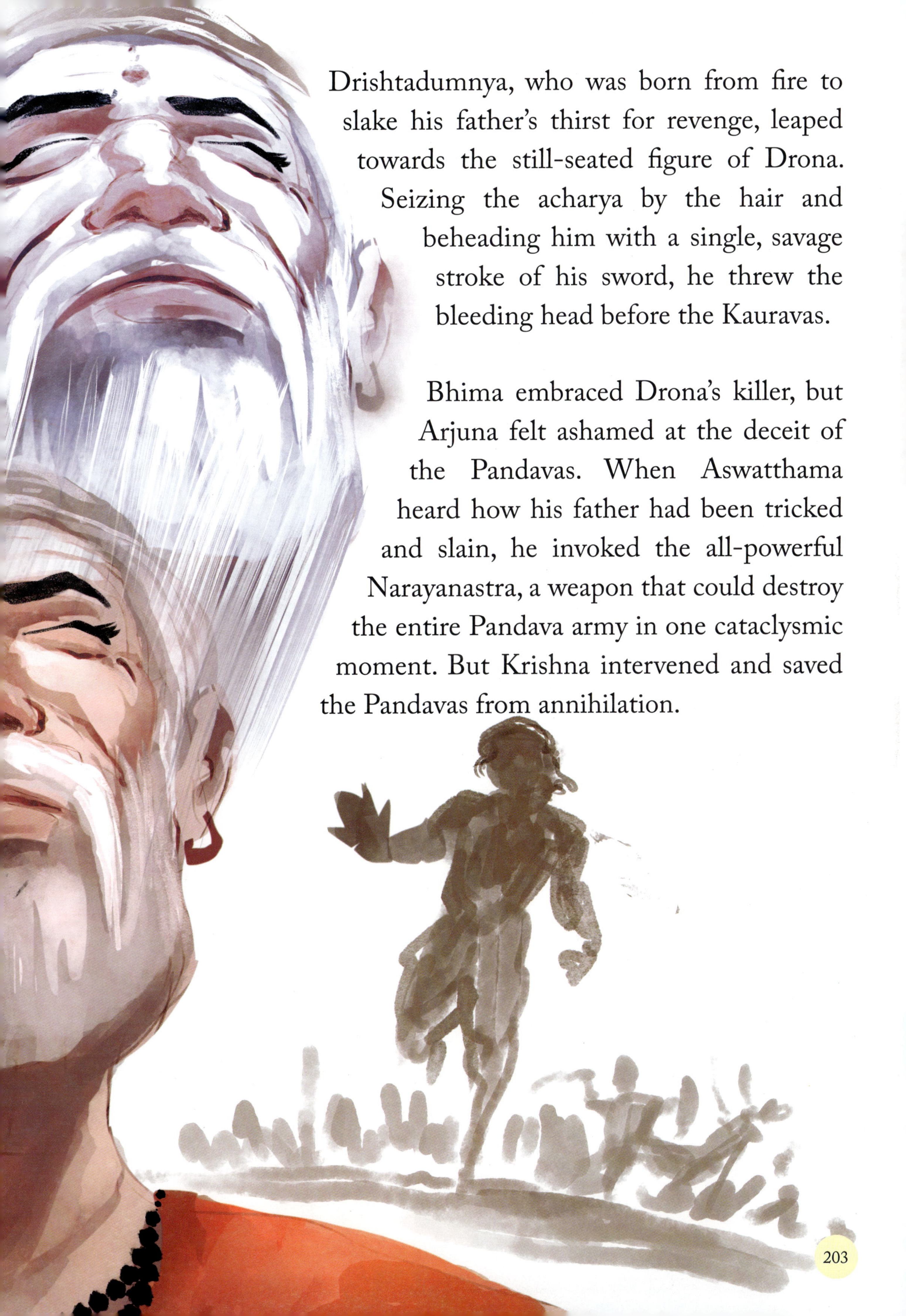

Drishtadumnya, who was born from fire to slake his father's thirst for revenge, leaped towards the still-seated figure of Drona. Seizing the acharya by the hair and beheading him with a single, savage stroke of his sword, he threw the bleeding head before the Kauravas.

Bhima embraced Drona's killer, but Arjuna felt ashamed at the deceit of the Pandavas. When Aswatthama heard how his father had been tricked and slain, he invoked the all-powerful Narayanastra, a weapon that could destroy the entire Pandava army in one cataclysmic moment. But Krishna intervened and saved the Pandavas from annihilation.

# 15. The Death of Karna

After Acharya Drona's death, Karna assumed command of the Kaurava forces. Armed with Vijaya, a gold-plated bow crafted for the gods, the proud warrior rode his shining chariot into the battlefield with all the majesty and splendor of the rising sun.

The battleground of Kurukshetra bore the fury of another long day of bloodshed. One by one, Karna had faced all the Pandavas except Arjuna in single combat. Remembering his promise to Kunti, he had spared their lives. The decisive battle would be fought between him and Arjuna. On the seventeenth day of the war, Karna confronted the likelihood of his own death with calmness and courage.

Salya, the king of Madra and the maternal uncle of Nakula and Sahadeva—was his charioteer. When war was declared, he came from Madra with his army to join the Pandavas. But Duryodhana wooed him en route with lavish hospitality, and he agreed to fight for the Kauravas. His loyalty however remained with the Pandavas.

Scorning Karna as an upstart, Salya became his charioteer only at Duryodhana's express request. He continuously taunted Kunti's firstborn son. But as the war went on, Karna's valor won Salya over. That afternoon, as Arjuna's chariot rushed towards them, he spoke words of encouragement that brought tears to Karna's eyes.

Before Karna and Arjuna could confront each other, there was a fierce fight between Dussasana and Bhima. For a while, their strengths were evenly matched. Then Bhima hurled Dussasana to the ground with a powerful blow of his mace. As the injured Kaurava lay writhing, all the indignities that Draupadi had suffered crowded Bhima's mind and maddened him. Like a wild beast, he leaped on Dussasana, tore open his breast and drank the blood from it. As he raised his blood-smeared face from the corpse, he shouted with joy, and all those who saw him—both friends and foes—were shaken.

For Karna and Arjuna the fateful hour had come. Their clash shook the three worlds. Sharp-edged arrows crisscrossed the sky like streaks of lightning, and the twang of the two mighty bows, the Gandiva and the Vijaya, resounded over Kurukshetra.

Karna fitted a deadly serpent shaft to his bow and aimed it at Arjuna's neck. The Nagastra sped hissing towards its target. Krishna averted the attack by forcing the horses to kneel and lowering the chariot. The arrow shattered the crown on Arjuna's head but spared his life.

All of a sudden, the left wheel of Karna's chariot got stuck in the soft earth. Leaving Salya to control the horses, Karna jumped down to pull the wheel out of the mud.

'Wait, Arjuna!' he cried as he heaved and tugged at the wheel. 'Do not shoot. I am unarmed. Remember the rules of battle.'

'Abhimanyu, too, was unarmed when you killed him. You did not remember the rules of battle then.' Krishna's harsh words brought a flush of shame to Karna's cheeks. At that moment, he desperately tried to invoke the Brahmastra, the divine weapon which was taught to him by Parasurama. But the curse that came along with it took effect. Just when Karna needed it the most, he could not remember the divine mantra.

As he strained to lift the wheel with both hands, Arjuna took aim. A crescent-shaped arrow—as sharp and swift as death—flew from the Gandiva, severing Karna's head from his body. Like a broken lotus, the beautiful head fell to the ground, and with it fell all hopes of victory for the Kauravas. Sadly, Surya the Sun God bade farewell to his unfortunate son, illumining and embracing the injured body with his rays. Blinded by tears, Salya rode the empty chariot away while the conches and trumpets of the Pandava army blared in triumph.

Karna's death broke the heart of his beloved friend Duryodhana. Seeing his grief, Acharya Kripa, Duryodhana's first guru, was moved to pity. 'Give up this senseless war,' he said. 'You cannot win this war, my son. So many great warriors slain, to what purpose? Make peace with your cousins, Duryodhana. Do not throw your life away.'

'Acharya, it is too late to talk of peace.' Duryodhana's eyes were red with grief. 'How can there be peace when a river of blood lies between us? I, alone, have caused so many deaths. Pitamaha Bhishma, Guru Drona, Jayadratha, Dussasana, Karna; all fought for me and fell. Is it befitting that I save myself when such great ones have perished for my sake? Let me die like a kshatriya on the battlefield and rejoin my comrades in heaven.'

Fortifying the remnants of his army with brave words, Duryodhana prepared once more for battle.

# 16. The End of the Kauravas

On the eighteenth day of the war, Duryodhana appointed Salya, commander-in-chief of the Kaurava forces. Salya, the king of Madra, thundered into battle with his men and a great massacre followed.

Grim-faced Yudhishthira fought with Salya for a long time. Neither of them gave up. Then, with all his strength, Yudhishthira hurled a sharp and shining spear, which went through Salya's body, killing him instantly.

Duryodhana's surviving brothers jointly attacked Bhima. And Bhima killed each one of them, except for Duryodhana.

The Kaurava army began to scatter in fear and confusion. Sakuni tried to control it as Sahadeva advanced. Sakuni fought the youngest Pandava, who had sworn to kill him after the infamous game of dice. Arrows flew through the air like poisoned darts, and the last one slashed through Sakuni's neck and killed him. Duryodhana's evil mentor was no more. The man responsible for the ruin of a noble house lay ruined and lifeless in the dust.

The Pandavas decimated the entire Kaurava army, except for four great warriors, Aswatthama, Acharya Kripa, Kritavarma, and Duryodhana. Separated from the other three, Duryodhana stumbled towards a pool of water and took refuge in it to cool and rest his tired body.

The Pandavas discovered his hiding place. 'Come out and fight, Duryodhana!' called Yudhishthira. 'Where is your pride, your honor? After killing so many warriors, are you yourself afraid to die?'

'Death holds no fear for me,' replied Duryodhana. 'Nor life any joy or pleasure now that all my loved comrades are dead. What should I fight for? I give you this empty and wasted world, Yudhishthira. Rule it. Enjoy it. It is yours.'

Yudhishthira's gentle eyes flashed fire. 'Your generosity does not move me, Duryodhana,' he said. 'A kshatriya does not ask for charity. And you have already lost the land you claim as your own. Fight like a brave warrior and retrieve your kingdom or die fighting and let your blood make amends for all your wrong deeds.'

Duryodhana rose out of the pool, his wounded body streaming blood.

'Feel free to choose your weapon and your opponent,' said the generous-hearted Yudhishthira. 'If you win, the kingdom is yours.'

Duryodhana chose the mace with which he could have defeated Yudhishthira, Arjuna, Nakula or Sahadeva. But scorning an unequal fight, he chose Bhima as his adversary.

Rivals and enemies since childhood, Duryodhana and Bhima clashed like two mighty bulls. Mace thudded against mace, and the earth trembled. The battle went on for a long time. Bhima was stronger, Duryodhana more agile. Their magnificent bodies were dripping sweat and blood as they grappled with each other, broke away, rested, and returned to the fight.

After the game of dice, Duryodhana had bared his thigh and invited Draupadi to sit on it, shaming her before the entire assembly. It was then that Bhima had sworn to smash Duryodhana's thighs, and kill Dussasana and drink his blood. So, the moment Duryodhana leaped up to avoid a blow, Bhima smashed the mace against his thighs and broke them. Duryodhana fell, writhing in pain.

Thus, both the terrible vows were fulfilled.

Devoid of all pomp and power, the last of the Kauravas lay dying in the dust. Bhima brandished his mace and kicked Duryodhana's head but Yudhishthira restrained him.

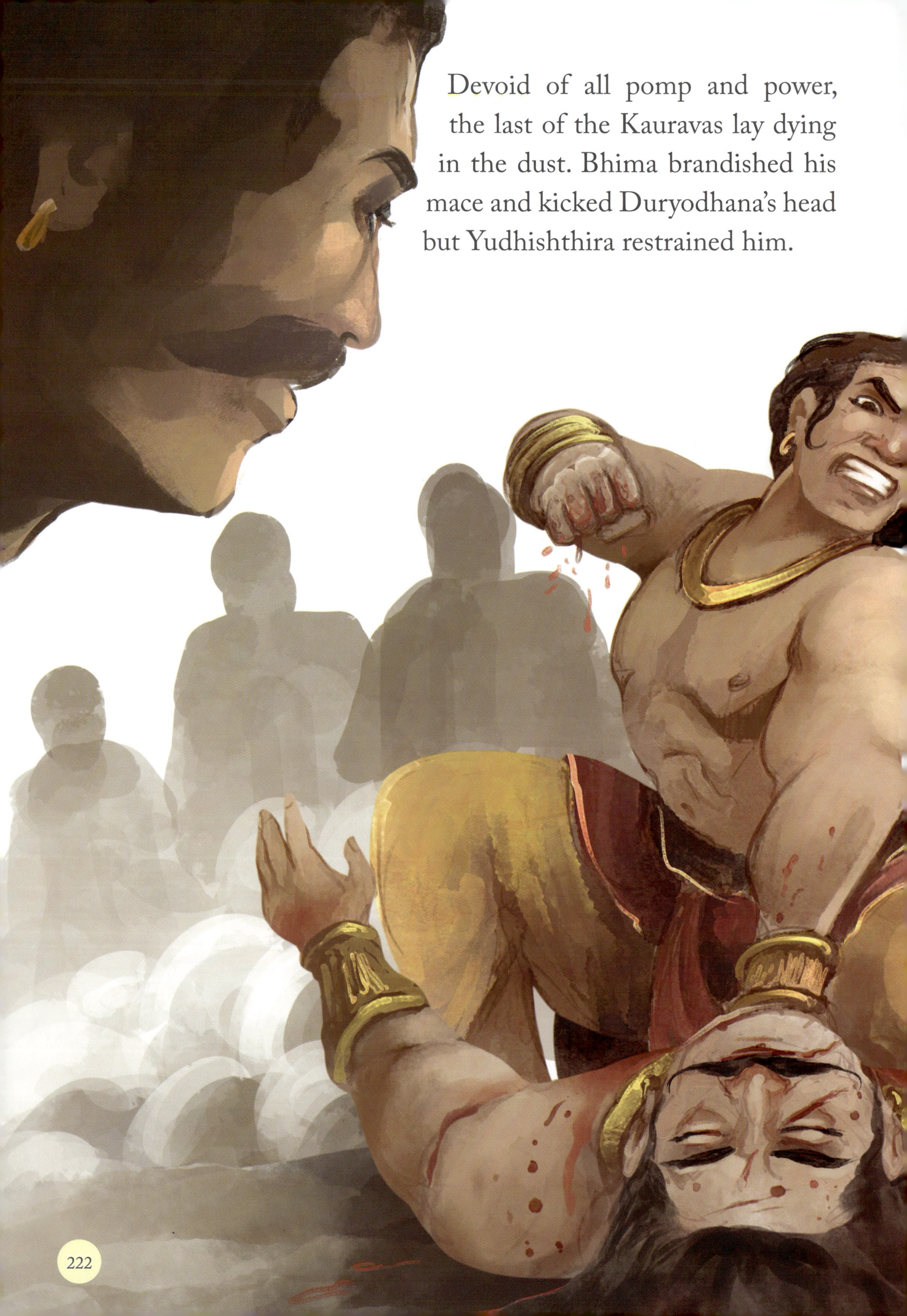

'Whatever he may have done, Duryodhana is a prince and our cousin. He has paid the ultimate penalty for his sins. Bhima, do not humiliate him further.'

'I do not mind,' said Duryodhana. 'I have lived a full and glorious life and I die, as every kshatriya would, bravely on the battlefield. Let Bhima place his foot upon my head. Soon will not vultures and crows do the same?'

The gods themselves applauded the courageous words of the dying prince and showered him with flowers. For all his faults and misdeeds, Duryodhana was a man of valor and he died like a brave soldier.

# 17. Yudhishthira's Coronation

The Pandavas left Duryodhana near the pool to die a lonely and painful death. It was there that the remaining warriors of the Kaurava army: Aswatthama, Acharya Kripa, and Kritavarma, found him and heard how he had been unfairly hit below the navel.

Anger flamed in Aswatthama's heart, and he swore to kill the Pandavas that very night. Duryodhana appointed him the commander-in-chief and wished him success.

During the night, Acharya Kripa, Kritavarma, and Aswatthama made their way to the Pandava camp. Drishtadyumna, Sikhandin, and all Draupadi's sons were asleep in their tents. Ruthlessly Aswatthama slew them all and then set fire to the camp. Except for Drishtadumnya's charioteer, all the Pandava soldiers died.

The Pandavas along with Krishna, had spent the night in the camp of the vanquished Kauravas. Drishtadumnya's charioteer brought them the terrible news of the massacre. It was the cruelest blow and for a while, it shattered them. As Draupadi wept over the bodies of her sons, the Pandavas set out in search of Aswatthama.

After a long and tiring search, they found him hiding among the disciples of Sage Vyasa on the bank of the Ganga. Acharya Kripa had returned to Hastinapur, and Kritavarma had gone back to his kingdom. Aswatthama saw the Pandavas approaching. He knew they were too powerful for him to slay. Therefore he attempted to wipe out the race of the Pandavas by killing Abhimanyu's unborn son in the womb of his mother, Uttara. He invoked the deadliest divine weapons that his father Drona had taught him to use. Krishna brought the unborn baby back to life, and Aswatthama fled into the forest, doomed to wander forever guilt-ridden and alone.

In Hastinapur, broken-hearted Dhritarashtra mourned the death of his sons. Supported by his father, Sage Vyasa, his brother Vidura and faithful Sanjaya, who had narrated to him all that had happened in the eighteen days of the war, the blind monarch proceeded towards the battlefield of Kurukshetra. The two queens, Gandhari and Kunti, and thousands of bereaved women followed the king, weeping for their loved ones.

Krishna and the Pandavas met Dhritarashtra outside the city. Yudhishthira bent to touch his feet, and the blind king embraced him half-heartedly. Then it was Bhima's turn. As Dhritarashtra opened his arms to greet the slayer of his sons, quick as a flash,

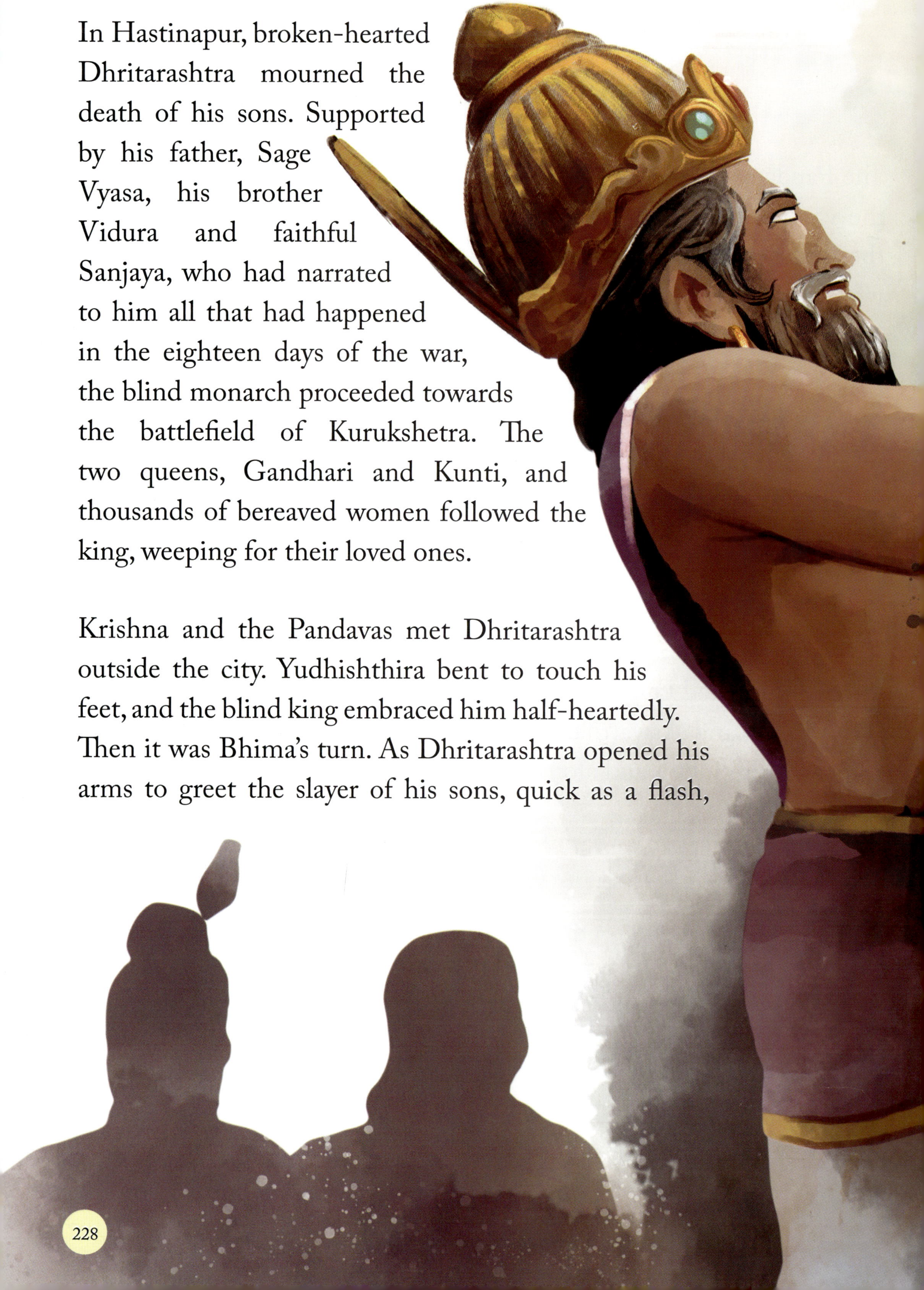

Krishna placed an iron statue of Bhima in the blind king's embrace. Dhritarashtra's powerful arms tightened around the figure. As the painful memory of all that Bhima had done seared his heart, he crushed the iron figure to fragments. The next instant, he collapsed, blood flowing from his lacerated chest.

'I have killed my brother's son,' he moaned. 'My anger led me to this foul deed.'

'Bhima is alive,' Krishna said gently. 'Great king, you are wise and learned. Do not blame the sons of Pandu for the retribution that your sons brought upon themselves for their misdeeds.'

Chastened, Dhritarashtra embraced his nephews, and his tears mingled with theirs. Noble Gandhari controlling her grief, blessed the Pandavas and consoled Draupadi, who too had lost all her children.

The dead were cremated and the last rites were performed on the banks of the river Ganga. Kunti then revealed the secret of Karna's identity that had tormented her for so long.

The Pandavas were stunned as well as overcome by anguish. They had reviled the brother they would have worshipped had they known his identity. They had killed him, whom they should have given their lives to protect.

Yudhishthira recalled the game of dice. Burning with shame and anger, he had sat with his eyes lowered as the Kauravas insulted Draupadi. Suddenly he had seen Karna's feet and his anger had melted away. Karna's feet were just like Kunti's. Now he knew why. The truth was heartbreaking.

Sorrowfully, the Pandavas bade farewell to the brother they had gained only by losing him. Full of grief and guilt, Yudhishthira lost all interest in the kingdom, won after so much bloodshed. He decided to renounce kingship and retire to the forest as an ascetic to do penance for his sins.

His brothers pleaded with him not to take such a drastic step. Krishna and Sage Vyasa tried to calm Yudhishthira's troubled soul with words of wisdom. 'Set your grief aside,' they said. 'The war is over. The kshatriyas that died in battle are now in heaven. Cease to mourn them and take up your duties as a king. The wise and noble Bhishma is still alive. With his guidance, rule Hastinapur well and fulfill your destiny.'

Before assuming the duties of a king, Yudhishthira went to Bhishma Pitamaha, who lay on the bed of arrows, waiting for the sun to begin his journey northwards. Gently, Krishna cleared the great Kuru elder's mind of fatigue and pain. Refreshed and pain-free by the grace of the Lord, Bhishma answered all Yudhishthira's questions and guided him in the duties of a righteous king. He showed Yudhishthira the path of dharma that men of virtue must follow to achieve salvation, and Yudhishthira imbibed his words like drops of nectar.

It was time for Bhishma to release himself from the bondage of his life on earth. Dhritarashtra, Gandhari, Kunti, Yudhishthira, and his brothers, Krishna, Vyasa, Vidura, and many holy men and citizens of Hastinapur gathered around him to pay their last respects.

Bhishma turned his tired eyes towards Krishna. 'Grant me leave to go, my lord,' he said.

'Noblest of men, death awaits your summons. Free yourself from this life of pain and return to your heavenly abode forever.' Krishna revealed himself in all his divinity to the dying man.

Blessed by the radiance of the Lord, Bhishma willed himself to die. His spirit ascended to the heavens like a glowing meteor. And the air was filled with the fragrance of many flowers. The heavens rejoiced in Bhishma's homecoming, as the people of Hastinapur reverentially placed the body of the beloved patriarch on his funeral pyre.

Putting sorrow and regret behind him, Yudhishthira returned to Hastinapur. With due honor and ceremony, and the holy chanting of Vedic mantras, Krishna seated Yudhishthira on the illustrious throne of the Kurus. His brothers and his uncle Vidura were with him to assist him in governing the kingdom.

# 18. Pandavas' Journey to Heaven

Yudhishthira followed the path of dharma and became an ideal king. Fifteen peaceful and prosperous years went by before the old and blind Dhritarashtra decided to leave Hastinapur and live his remaining days in penance and meditation in the forest.

Yudhishthira was very unhappy on hearing this. He had given Dhritarashtra utmost love and respect, consulted him on every issue, and ministered to all his needs. Though he loved Yudhishthira in return and reproached himself for the injustice done to the Pandavas, the old king still mourned for his sons and knew no peace of mind.

Sadly, the Pandavas let him go. Gandhari, Vidura, Sanjaya, and Kunti accompanied him.

'Do not stop me,' Kunti said to her sons. 'Let me do as my heart and duty dictate. Your future is at last secure, and you know my blessings are always with you. May you live long, righteous, and prosperous lives!'

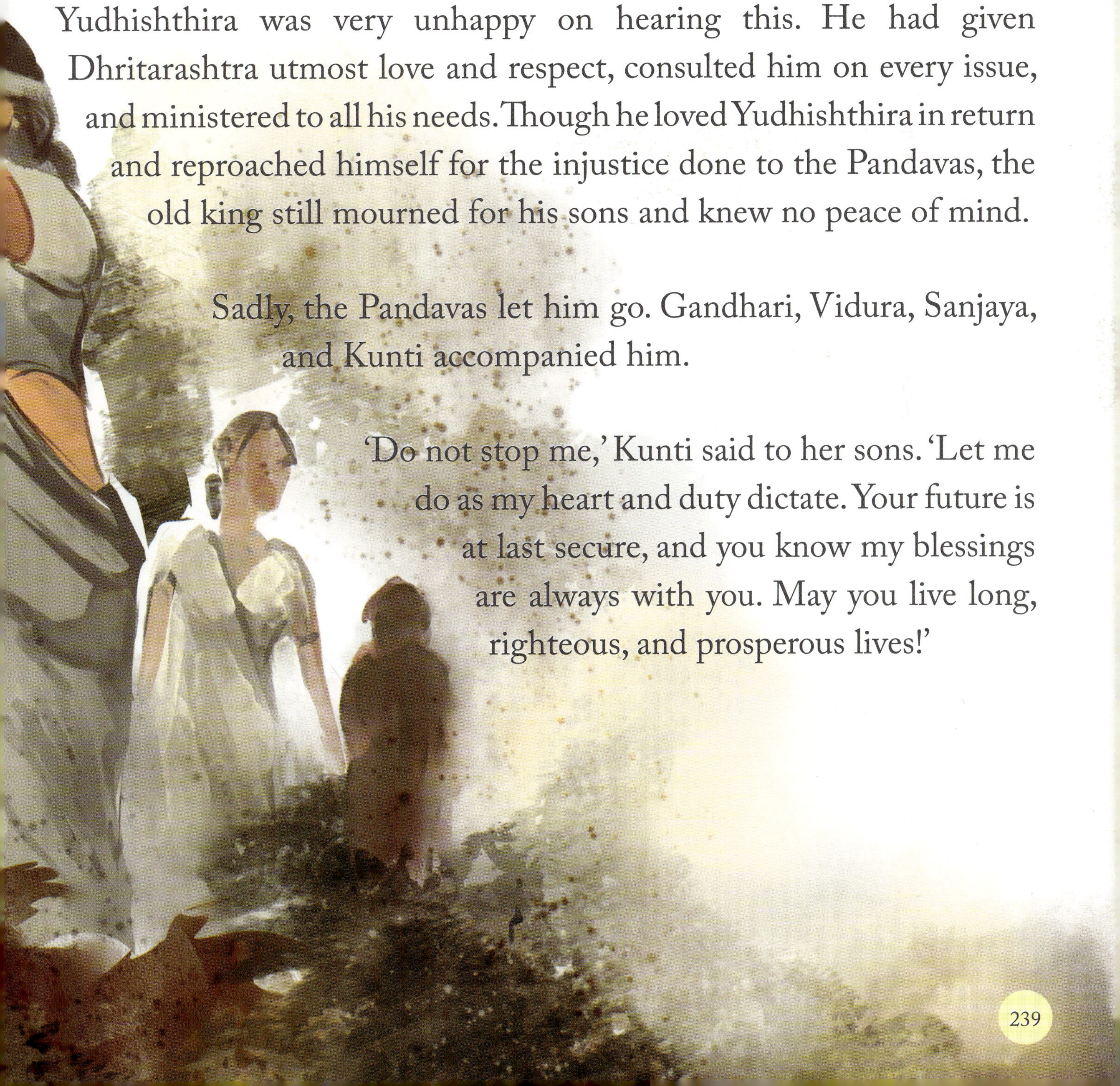

The elders of the Kuru house walked slowly and serenely towards the forest. The people of Hastinapur bid them farewell with heavy hearts. Three years later, death claimed them in the guise of a forest fire. Vidura, too, gave up his life, and Sanjaya spent the rest of his days as an ascetic in the high mountains.

'In age after age, whenever evil threatens to engulf the world, I come to protect the good and establish dharma.' Lord Krishna said this to Arjuna at the beginning of the great war. With the overthrow of the Kauravas and the restoration of truth and justice—the Lord's mission had been fulfilled.

Thirty-six years after the coronation of Yudhishthira, Krishna relinquished his mortal frame, allowing the arrow of a hunter to pierce his body. The divine radiance that illumined the lives of the Pandavas for so long returned to heaven, leaving them orphaned and desolate.

Yudhishthira gave up the throne and crowned Abhimanyu's son Parikshit as the king of Hastinapur. Parikshit was the Pandavas' only heir. Aswatthama's divine weapon had killed him while he was still in his mother's womb, but Krishna had restored him to life so that the race of the Pandavas could survive.

Leaving their kingdom secure, the Pandavas renounced the world. Dressed like ascetics, they set out on their final journey together. They reached the Himalayas after visiting many holy places and toiled up the high mountain peak of Meru. Draupadi was the first to collapse and die. Sahadeva died next, followed by Nakula, Arjuna, and Bhima. Yudhishthira continued to toil upwards, accompanied only by a dog that had followed the Pandavas all along their journey.

Then in a great burst of light, Indra Deva descended from heaven in his chariot. 'Come, Yudhishthira,' he said. 'Your time on earth has ended. Come with me to the heaven you richly deserve. Your brothers and Draupadi are already there, waiting for you. They have discarded their earthly bodies. But you will enter heaven as you are now. Come.'

'My lord, allow me to take this dog,' said Yudhishthira. 'He has long been my faithful companion.'

'There is no place for him in heaven,' said Lord Indra. 'Abandon him.'

'I cannot,' said Yudhishthira. 'Even if it means I must forsake the joys of heaven. How can I abandon a creature who has looked to me for protection?'

As he said these words, the dog vanished, and in its place stood Dharmaraja, great God of Dharma, and Yudhishthira's father.

'My son, I took the form of the dog to test you,' he said. 'Just as I tested you in the twelfth year of your exile when your wise answers to my questions brought your brothers back to life. Your nobility and compassion are unequaled on this earth. Come with me now to heaven.'

In the chariot of the gods, Yudhishthira rose to heaven. There, surrounded by the greatest kings who had ever ruled on earth, he saw Duryodhana seated in splendor. However, there was no sign of the Pandavas and Draupadi.

Anger seized Yudhishthira. 'I cannot stay in a heaven where a sinner like Duryodhana resides,' he said. 'Where are my brothers? Take me to them.'

'The rules of your world do not apply here,' the divine sage Narada spoke to Yudhishthira. 'Duryodhana lived and died like a fearless kshatriya. So he merits a place in heaven. Give up your anger and enmity.'

'Let me go to my brothers,' said the son of Dharmaraja. 'If Duryodhana is worthy of heaven, then where are they and countless other heroes who led lives of honor and courted death for my sake? Where are they all?'

'Take Yudhishthira to his brothers,' Lord Indra instructed his attendants. Yudhishthira followed as they led him out of heaven to a dark and foul-smelling region, slippery with blood from dismembered bodies and unimaginable filth.

Shaken and bewildered, Yudhishthira would have turned back when disturbing voices besieged him from all sides. 'Stay with us a little longer,' they cried. 'Your sweet presence relieves our agony.' Those voices were of the Pandavas, Karna, Draupadi, and her sons.

Yudhishthira's senses reeled. 'Go!' he cried to the attendants. 'If this is heaven's reward for those who followed dharma, then it is my reward as well. Return to Indra. I will stay here with my loved ones.'

Suddenly there was light and a calming and fragrant breeze blew away the stench of rotting flesh. All the gods appeared before Yudhishthira, radiant in their glory.

'Be comforted, my child,' said Dharmaraja. 'What you saw was only an illusion, designed to test your loyalty and adherence to truth. It was your third and final test. Do not fear for your loved ones. They await you in heaven, joyful and free of care. Shed this mortal frame and with it all the grief and torment of your earthly existence. Know your divinity, my son, and be at peace.'

So, at last, Yudhishthira was reunited with his loved ones, his comrades and kinsmen; with Karna, the brother he had never known on earth; with Duryodhana, whose brave spirit had been purged of all sin.

All was harmony and in the bliss of heaven, the wounds inflicted by the terrible battle of Kurukshetra were healed forever.